Save My Soul

Book 1 in the
Kemmons Brothers Baseball Series

Elley Arden

CRIMSON
ROMANCE
F+W Media, Inc.

Published by
Crimson Romance
an imprint of F+W Media, Inc.
10151 Carver Road, Suite 200
Blue Ash, Ohio 45242

www.crimsonromance.com

ISBN-10: 1-4405-6604-6
ISBN-13: 978-1-4405-6604-2
eISBN-10: 1-4405-6605-4
eISBN-13: 978-1-4405-6605-9

DEDICATION

To my soul mate, my husband, who believes in me, especially when I don't believe in myself.

ACKNOWLEDGMENTS

First and foremost, I'd like to thank Nicole Helm, fellow romance novelist and critique partner *extraordinaire*, who helped me spit and polish this manuscript until it turned into a book. Without her firm hand, I would've given up long ago.

My family and friends continually bless me with their love and support. Warm words of encouragement, easy hugs, and bottomless glasses of wine, got me through more doubt than they'll ever know.

And last but not least, I'm thankful for summer vacations spent in Lake Norman, North Carolina, where the sun soothes, the water calms, and the inspiration is endless.

CHAPTER ONE

Maggie blinked at the picture she held in her hand. She rubbed her eyes. She tilted her head. She even squinted. No matter how she studied the tattered square, the image didn't make sense.

Her date reached across the bistro table and flicked the back of the photo. "That's my wife and kids."

Maggie counted eight children. A PhD in counseling psychology couldn't guide her reaction. Years of embracing Buddhist dharma couldn't ease her shock.

"I'm sorry." She shook the fog from her brain. "You said ex-wife, right? I must've misheard you." Which wasn't likely. Psychotherapists knew how to listen.

A smile warmed Paul's brown eyes and brought out a dimple in his cheek. Maggie hadn't noticed the deep dip a week ago when he grinned from behind a farmer's market herb stand. She hadn't noticed a wedding ring, either. Glancing at his naked left hand, she felt relieved. There had to be a rational explanation for this irrational conversation.

"Katherine is my wife. We've been married for twenty years." The words leaped from his lips and pinned Maggie to her chair, snapping her bare back against the metal with enough force to sting.

She folded her arms over her chest and breathed, trying to plot a graceful exit from the alternative universe disguised as a coffee shop she must have landed in.

"It's time for another wife."

This was where desperation had led her. But as much as she loathed being a twenty-eight-year-old PhD living at home with her mother, Maggie wasn't desperate enough to escape by way of a married man. She might be liberal, forward-thinking, and even a little off-the-proverbial-wall, but she wasn't a home wrecker.

Drawing a shaky breath, she cursed the crowded location and leaned forward. "I'm sorry. You seem nice enough, but I can't be with a married man. Tonight was a mistake."

She reached into her patchwork purse, but before she fished out keys, Paul wrapped a clammy hand around her wrist. "Don't go. Let me explain. I have Katherine's blessing to pursue you."

"You don't have my permission," Maggie said, uninterested in the details.

He released her and slinked back in his chair, looking very much the misunderstood martyr with glassy eyes and tight lips.

A bolt of pity wrapped in sensibility struck her brain. *Deep breath, Maggie. Calm down.* After all, the evening was innocent. They hadn't even held hands. What harm had been done on a platonic first date?

Compassion caused her to smile. "Good night, Paul. Go home to your wife and kids."

"But I'm a polygamist. I want another wife, and Katherine wants a sister wife."

Maggie widened her eyes. Though rumor had it Salt Lake City overflowed with plural marriages, in the year since she'd moved home with Crystal, Maggie had yet to meet one. Until tonight.

Grabbing the edge of the cold table, she breathed through her nose and exhaled relief. Paul wasn't risking the wrath of karma by proposing an illicit affair. He was explaining an alternative lifestyle. While Maggie had no desire to be Wife Two, she owed him civility and the opportunity to communicate without humiliation. After all, she was an expert in interpersonal communication.

She nodded in understanding. "Please tell Katherine I'm sorry, but I'm not sister wife material. Thank you for the coffee."

Maggie lifted from the seat with as much grace as she could muster and scurried across the tile floor. Her feet wobbled in too-high heels, and her knees knocked below the hem of her flowing skirt. When she finally reached the exit, a cool rush of late October air layered her skin with goose pimples.

She'd been in a lot of ridiculous situations, but this may have topped them all.

Slamming the door of her Aquarius blue VW convertible, Maggie faced the fact that her date was a bust, and now she was going to have to drive home. Face her mother. Rehash the story when all she wanted to do was climb into bed.

This was not the life she expected to be living at twenty-eight. Then again, her entire life had been beyond normal expectations. When most mothers were teaching their daughters to read books, Maggie's mother was teaching her how to read auras. Inside their circle of friends, inside the safe haven of their bungalow, it was a skill no different than rolling her tongue. But out here, in mainstream society, it made Maggie weird, an outcast. She couldn't seem to fit in. Even the men she attracted were…different.

Maggie dropped her head to the steering wheel and groaned. Where was the balance? The ying and the yang? She'd worked hard to gain academic success and respect, in the process, hiding a big portion of herself and her upbringing. And where did that get her? Barely able to pay her student loan interest, car expenses and rent for her office space. This was "failure to launch" wasn't it? She was doomed to grow old, at home, alongside her aura-reading, spell-chanting mother.

But right now, Maggie couldn't go home. She couldn't face the woman who'd be waiting in the rocking chair. Sometimes a girl didn't need her mother.

She turned the key, firing the engine, not knowing where she was going. Her friends were polar opposites—spiritual seekers vs. mental health professionals—and yet both groups would agree Maggie was struggling with self-discovery. What Maggie really wanted was a single friend who would line up shots and drink with her to oblivion.

She drove without direction, listening to the pathetic thoughts in her head until she tired of the wallowing and replaced her thoughts with a mantra. She whispered the words over and over again as she traveled tree-lined streets. Eventually, her mouth stopped moving and thoughts started forming. The first? She had a decision to make. She couldn't live in both worlds. Either she embraced her mother's way of life or she moved out and carved life on her own. But between student loans, car expenses, and rent for her mostly unused office space, Maggie had only managed to save five hundred dollars since she moved back home. It wasn't enough money for a security deposit, let alone a down payment.

Passing her street, needing more time to think, Maggie guided the car down South Temple and stopped to let a ghost and goblin cross. In the chaos of the evening, she'd forgotten about Halloween. Glancing at her white knuckles, she wished she was younger, with hands wrapped around a pillowcase bursting with candy instead of strangling a steering wheel. Kids didn't know how hard life would get. They couldn't imagine there would ever come a time when they wanted to move out of the house and live life on their own. But Maggie knew, and knowing sucked.

With no other place to go, Maggie parked her Volkswagen in the driveway of a historic Victorian, disarmed security features at the back door and reset the system on the other side. She switched on a chandelier in the main hall and blinked at the brightness. Crystal always said, *look for the bright side*, but Maggie couldn't find a bright side when she was in the middle of an existential crisis.

She growled as she pounded her heels against the hardwoods and took the wool-covered stairs by two. At the east end of the wallpapered hall, she ducked into her office, shutting the six-panel door and driving a bolt lock into place. For a moment, she froze against the thick wood, but then an exhale carried her lanky body to a purple couch. She collapsed, face down on the purple velvet. Reaching up without looking, Maggie switched on a glitzy lamp and turned her head. She opened her eyes to the Buddha that Crystal had placed against the far wall and the tapestry zafu that was a graduation present from Yogi Hajan. The pair would no doubt advise Maggie to meditate, but she couldn't muster an ounce of spiritual motivation. She looked away before the inanimate objects could guilt her further.

Her orange Macbook sat on the desk where she'd left it hours ago after a virtual therapy session. Maybe one of "her girls" needed help. Somehow it was easier helping other people face their emotional, spiritual, and familial crises than it was helping herself.

Maggie booted the computer and headed straight for Facebook. No new messages. Nothing lurked in her inbox either. Of course not. What sort of college kid stayed in and chatted with her therapist on Halloween night when there were fraternity mixers and costume parties to attend?

She typed a quick email to the small group of clients, detailing her open availability tomorrow. Via email, chat room, webcam or old-fashioned telephone, Maggie would listen to stories of binge-eating peanut butter cups and the bouts of purging that kept the troubled young women up all night.

Pain twisted her heart, and this time the hurt wasn't because of her own screwy life. Virtual therapy allowed Maggie to guide eight clients, battling eating disorders in different corners of the country. The technique was her focus in graduate school, earning her name recognition in scholarly journals near and far. Her avant-garde approach to therapy was something to be proud of, the one and only time she was able to mesh her alternative side with her professional side, resulting in vigorous accolades.

Maggie ran shaky fingers through her spiky hair and considered meditating again, but her thoughts were hijacked by a ringing cell phone. She blinked at the touch screen, expecting to see Crystal or even Polygamist Paul, not an unknown number. The twist of her stomach told her not to answer, but her brain overrode the unexplained nervousness. What if someone was in trouble?

"Maggie Collins," she answered.

There was a brief pause, followed by the deep rumble of a throat clearing. "Dr. Collins, this is Jordon Kemmons. I'm not sure if you remember me."

Her core temperature plunged and then skyrocketed. The skin on her arms pimpled, and tingles spread across her chest. "I remember."

How could she forget? Six months ago, his tan skin, black hair, towering stature, and ominous aura haunted her from behind the podium, where he addressed the graduating class of his alma mater—now her alma mater, too. He stirred such strong feelings in Maggie, she worried the neo-gothic buildings surrounding the commons would crumble after more than one hundred years of steadfast footing. But that was nothing compared to the unsettling jolt of their shared handshake when Maggie was awarded recognition for her research. Something about the darkly handsome man strangled her breath and drained her soul.

"I hope it's not too late to call. I work all hours and pay little attention to clocks and time zones. Can you talk or should we set another time?"

He didn't sound the least bit remorseful for the intrusion, and she had the intuitive feeling that he intended to have the discussion whether she was busy or not. A burst of nervous energy fluttered between her ribs.

"I happen to be at the office, so it's the perfect time to talk." About anything other than late-twenties life crises or polygamists and sister wives.

Maggie ditched her red heels and folded her long legs in the shape of a pretzel.

"You see patients on Halloween night?"

"Clients." How many times had Maggie explained to the layperson about the importance of choosing words wisely when it came to mental health? She sighed and reached for a rote explanation. "The word patient denotes sickness, and my clients aren't sick. They need options and guidance. And no, I'm not seeing clients. I'm doing...inner work."

Silence. She leaned forward, carrying goose-pimpled arms to her knees where her eyes caught the movement of a nickel-sized spider suspended from the blade of a ceiling fan.

"Dr. Collins, I have a proposition for you."

The spider plummeted toward her bare leg. She screamed and leaped across the room, panting into the phone.

"What?" he barked. "Are you all right?" His yelling vibrated her eardrum and flooded her body with foolishness.

She kept her eyes on the spider and one hand over her throbbing heart. "I'm fine. It's a spider." She drew a deep, cleansing breath. "I apologize for my skittishness tonight."

"Let me guess. You believe portals to the other dimension open at midnight on All Hallows Eve, populating the earth with immortals hungry for human souls."

Maggie balked. Was this guy serious? He had no idea how scary real life could be. "Immortals haven't even crossed my mind, Mr. Kemmons. I'm merely distracted with thoughts of polygamy, sister wives and the likelihood of nervous breakdowns in a person's mid-twenties."

More silence. Deeper silence. The kind that made a heartbeat echo.

The spider scurried up the arm of the sofa and then made a U-turn toward the floor. Maggie leaped onto a leopard print footstool.

"Dr. Collins, I'm the agent for a pitcher who flaked out during game six of the NLCS. My sports psychologists can't break through. I don't think he's eating, and I've noticed unexplainable scars on his arms. Obviously this isn't about pitching. The kid is crazy, but his high-profile image makes it difficult to seek inpatient treatment without career repercussions. Remembering your research, I thought maybe you could help."

Maggie winced and dug emerald green toe nails into the cushion, once again taking on the role as champion for the misunderstood. "Mr. Kemmons, the terms 'flaked out' and 'crazy' are offensive. People on a tormented mental plane don't deserve to have their temporary weaknesses belittled."

"Call him whatever you want to call him. I'll call it like I see it. And the way I see it, he isn't focusing. He can't throw a strike, and his fast ball dropped eight miles per hour. I can't negotiate a case of bats for him at that speed."

The spider disappeared under the sofa and reappeared on the woodwork. Maggie dropped her butt to the footstool and pinned her eyes on the eight-legged creature.

"I've exhausted all legitimate, medical treatments," he said with a huff. "Next up is reiki and some cranial sacral voodoo that a team trainer suggested. Before I toss Carlos off the deep end and jump after him, I figured I'd give your brand of hocus pocus a try."

Maggie winced. If he wanted the best hocus pocus money could buy, he'd have to call her mother.

Reaching up to calm a twitching vein in her forehead, Maggie rubbed her clammy skin. "I don't even know where to start," she said, releasing a sigh. "Reiki and cranial sacral therapy *are* legitimate treatments, neither of which do I practice. My brand of hocus pocus…" she choked a little on the words, "…is nothing more than tradition therapy offered in a non-traditional format. I'm sorry to disappoint you, but while I feel sorry for this boy, and not because he isn't pitching well enough but because he's forced to deal with your spiritual retardation, I'm hardly the person to help him heal."

Jordon snorted. "Did you just call me retarded?"

Maggie rolled her eyes, going over her words in her head. "Of course not. I simply meant your spiritual evolution is delayed."

"Is it now?" He didn't sound impressed.

She was beyond caring about impressions. Taking out the evening's frustrations on this faceless man seemed infinitely more enjoyable than beating herself up about it.

With a noisy exhale, Maggie released the frustration that had been locked inside of her since her awkward date with Paul. "Mr. Kemmons, every other word that comes out of your mouth offends me, and that's amazing, because I assure you, you won't find a more open-minded individual than me." She should've stopped there, but the emotional floodgate slammed open. "Just because I won't participate in a polygamist marriage or engage in orgiastic relationships doesn't mean I judge those who do."

Deep laughter slithered through the phone, tickling her ears and neck until it shot off tiny sparks in her chest. She pounded a fist against her breastbone to stop the tingles.

"Orgiastic." The way he said the word made her face burn. "I had no idea that was even a word."

She raised her hand, fanning the heat. "Never mind. I…Good night, Mr. Kemmons."

"Wait," he yelled. "I'm prepared to double your salary."

She didn't have a salary. She worked off billing and sliding scales. It was "eat what you kill," so to speak. And with her brand of therapy in low-demand, Maggie was starving.

"Dr. Collins, are you still there?"

Another shaky breath. "I am."

"Carlos plays for Carolina, and he's staying at my vacation home in Lake Norman. I'd like to pay you for a professional visit. Talk to him. See if you can help. Travel and hotel expenses will be covered."

For a moment, all Maggie could see was a couple days away from a life that was closing in on her, and some extra cash to start anew.

But when she opened her mouth to agree, her stomach clenched. If only she didn't feel like she was making a deal with the devil...

The spider scrambled in the distance, and Maggie scooted the footstool closer to the door.

"Are you interested in the opportunity, Dr. Collins?" he asked in a clipped and clearly exasperated tone.

Maggie had never been one to ignore opportunity, partly because she had her mother's impulsive streak, but also because she was smart and determined...and right now, she was struggling to make sense of her life. This opportunity could be key.

"Send me the terms in writing." She spewed the sentence before she could take it back, using as much conviction as she could muster.

The spider raced toward the footstool, and Maggie screamed, skipping across the hardwoods on tiptoes before she crashed into the sofa.

"What now?" he growled.

"The spider." She panted, waiting for the eight-legged demon to regroup and charge again.

"Kill the damn thing."

"No! That robs us of the chance to grow on a spiritual path. I practice a non-harming way of life, and I'm going to deal with this arachnophobia like any other enlightened adult. When I hang up, I'll talk to him."

Dead silence mixed with the distinct feeling that she said something wrong. Maggie knew the words that made sense to her sounded strange to everyone else—especially tall, dark, analytical men, but she couldn't help herself. Try as she might to tame her alternative thoughts, in times of duress they overruled.

She fought the urge to hang up and handle her mortification in private. "Mr. Kemmons, are you there?"

"I'm *all there*. I was about to ask you the same thing."

She caught his dreadful double meaning, but couldn't blame him. After all, she told him she planned to spend Halloween night talking to a spider.

Palming her face, she drew a deep breath and refocused. "You may think of my person however you like, but professionally, I'm without reproach. I accept your verbal terms and await a contract." He chuckled. "Good night, Dr. Collins. Give my regards to the spider."

*

Jordon pulled square black eyeglasses off his face and pressed his head to the scrolled headboard his interior decorator designed for occasions like this. He worked a lot in bed. There was a time when the work related to his libido. These days, the only thing waking him was the BlackBerry charging on his bamboo nightstand or the cordless phone resting in his hand.

A few feet below his bedroom window, the New York City streets hummed, keeping him company through another long night. He bent his knees, bringing the laptop with Carlos Nunez's final stats closer to his burning eyes and pressed the phone to his ear.

The buzzing was displaced by one word, spoken dejectedly with a hint of Spanish accent. "Hallow."

"Hey, buddy. How are you feeling tonight?"

"The same."

Jordon squeezed his lips until they hurt. When Carlos sniffed on the other end, Jordon thought about hopping a flight to Carolina so the kid didn't have to suffer alone. "Is Bernie there?"

"Just left." A yawn filtered through the receiver.

"Okay. Try to get some rest while I work on Plan B." Or was it Plan Z at this point?

Jordon smacked his head against the bed. If he had to, he'd start all over at Plan A and rework every detail until somebody, somewhere, helped this kid. "Night, buddy."

"Night…"

Dad. Jordon couldn't remember when it first happened, but for years now—maybe since he started down the hill toward forty—the name appeared in his head at the end of certain calls. For many of the young men he represented, the moniker wasn't far off. Jordon did more than guide their careers, and he sure as hell felt more for them than the average agent, which was precisely why Kemmons Corp. was anything but average.

Studying the laptop screen again, Jordon shook his head at the numbers. Last season, Carlos flaked out, but the kid wasn't a genuine flake, not like Dr. Maggie Collins.

You may think of my person however you like. Jordon clicked another browser tab and gazed on the exotic Maggie. Betty Boop eyes smiled at him from the pages of her website. He pushed a palm up the stubby underside of his chin, and a devilish grin crept across his lips. Oh, he liked. A lot.

The first time he saw her, she floated down a red carpet aisle, wrapped in traditional graduation garb—with the exception of those damn shoes. It took him a moment to remember he was presenting a doctoral award of excellence to the woman in fuck-me pumps. Later in the evening, at a graduate reception, they shook hands during an introduction, and Jordon momentarily lost his mind.

Glancing at his opening and closing hand, Jordon recalled the heat that travelled from her body to his. The physical attraction intensified when she joined a group in a belly-dancing tribute to an Egypt-bound professor. Having shed the scholarly robe, she wore a sleeveless dress that was little more than a slip. He remembered the generous amount of shapely leg between the hem of that so-called dress and the black bows tied around each ankle. Those tiny bows strapped stiletto heels to her feet as she rolled and swirled all over the dance floor like an erotic dream.

A dream he couldn't shake.

Snapping the laptop shut and tossing it to Bethany's side of the bed, Jordon slid down the headboard, pushed into the pillow and closed his eyes. The right side hadn't been Bethany's side for two years. He thought about rolling over, about reclaiming the space, but his back glued to the mattress. It pissed him off that he still couldn't sleep on the right side.

Maybe Carlos wasn't the only one who needed a therapist.

Jordon launched an exhale from his mouth to the ceiling. If Dr. Collins succeeded in fixing Carlos, maybe Jordon would modify his impression of her from flake to capable flake. The corners of his sleepy mouth lifted. Right now, though, the only impression he cared to imagine was how capable Dr. Maggie Collins was in bed.

CHAPTER TWO

Maggie's mother wore flowers in her hair; a wreath of pink alyssum set atop Crystal's gray, shoulder-length curls. Sitting cross-legged on Maggie's bed, Crystal looked like the Earth Mother, and Maggie loved her.

There was much to admire about Crystal. As a successful singer-songwriter in the seventies, pockets of fans lingered. The woman epitomized unconditional love and unadulterated passion. Most everything Maggie knew about the world, she learned from the petite whirlwind of positive energy.

"Oh, Magpie, those boots. Nothing good can come from wearing slaughtered calf."

But there were negatives, too.

Maggie folded a silk blouse and tucked it beside the Frye boots in question. The contradictory parts of Maggie cringed from guilt, and she rattled off a silent prayer of thanks to the cow who lost his life to create such magnificent footwear.

"Give me your palms." Crystal reached for her.

Normally Maggie wouldn't think twice, but lately her thoughts had been so troubling, she worried about Crystal's reaction if she knew. "My palms are packing."

Crystal seemed to take the rejection in stride, dropping her hands to a tangle of beads and thread littering her lap. "You're stressing, Magpie, and that's not a good way to embark on a journey. What's worrying you?"

Where to start? Every sunrise brought with it another contradiction in Maggie that didn't make sense. How could she explain that everything was worrying her? She looked at her mother and smiled. "I'm fine. I'm just trying to decide what to pack. Can you pass me my jewelry pouch?"

Crystal turned her attention from threading a green bead to the tightly wound tapestry pouch. "Is the travel amulet in here? You should have it on."

Maggie pulled a long silver chain from the scoop neck of her peasant blouse. She dangled an oversized pewter circle carved with alchemical and zodiac symbols in front of Crystal.

"Good girl. Safe passage can't be taken for granted. When you get there, wear the fourth pentacle of Mercury. You can never have too much knowledge and understanding of a new situation."

Maggie nestled the necklace between her bumps for breasts and the jewelry bag next to the dead cow's skin. She sighed, wanting to believe in knowledge and understanding she might gain from a piece of metal, but doubt was all around her. This was one of those times when she wished for someone to rub her back, smooth her hair, and say, "Everything will be okay."

Crystal wasn't that kind of mother.

"You're shutting me out." Crystal trained shiny green eyes on Maggie's face as if she could read her mind. "Why?"

"I'm not shutting you out," Maggie said, looking away.

"You've been distant for days."

"I've been preoccupied with work." It was the truth. Mostly.

As Maggie folded a pair of True Religion jeans across the top of the suitcase, Crystal gathered her beads.

"If space is what you want, Magpie, I'll give you space. Goddess knows I don't want your bad juju affecting me." Crystal hummed her way out of the room.

There would be plenty of space with Maggie in North Carolina. And there'd be even more space once Maggie moved out of her mother's home. Maybe then, when Maggie was finally, fully independent, she would know peace.

With a huff, Maggie zipped the suitcase and pulled it to the floor. Living here seemed like the answer to Maggie's student-loan-riddled prayers, and at first, the arrangement wasn't bad, especially when

Crystal traveled. But the first time one of Crystal's trips turned into a disappearance, Maggie was thrust into the maternal role, searching, worrying, praying for Crystal to keep safe. After years of enduring Crystal's randomness, Maggie should've been immune, but she wasn't, and a piece of paper declaring Maggie a mental health professional didn't help her come to terms with her mother's extremes.

A distorted image bounced back at Maggie from the suitcase's shiny surface. One look and she was struck by how little she resembled Crystal. Maggie was long and straight, while Crystal was small and rounded. So many dominant genes raced through Maggie's body that over the years she thought about searching for her father. She imagined him being a giant, because her size nine feet and nearly six foot frame couldn't be a random joke of nature. But Crystal wasn't receptive to sharing information with Maggie, and a search would span continents.

Like it or not, sometimes it was best to leave the past alone.

Tucking an envelope with her ticket and itinerary into the front pocket, Maggie zipped her suitcase. The flight to Charlotte departed just after eight in the morning, and following a stop in Chicago, arrived before five. Jordon said a car would be waiting at the airport to drive her forty-five minutes north to Lake Norman.

She was packed. Her bank account was fattened with a partial, upfront payment. And her future waited. So why couldn't Maggie shake the worry?

"Magpie, you have visitors."

*

Paul stood in the foyer hand in hand with a woman who looked like the stereotypical librarian, complete with thick-rimmed glasses and mousy brown hair pulled into a bun. An oversized T-shirt strained across fleshy breasts and fell over the waistband of a pair of khaki pants.

"Love and goodness, friends. Please, come in."

Maggie watched Paul and the woman she assumed to be his wife follow Crystal into the cottage kitchen.

"This is a surprise," Maggie said, clearing the dry shock from her throat.

Paul lifted the woman's hand and patted. "I'm sorry for barging in, but I wanted to introduce you to Katherine. We were hoping that if you spent some time with both of us, your feelings would be less negative."

Maggie's throat closed. She looked at the quiet woman who neither smiled nor frowned, her thin lips forming a noncommittal line and her eyes glazing over, like she waited for commands from a universal remote. The subservient image sent a shiver up Maggie's spine.

"I don't feel anything negative toward either of you," Maggie stammered. "I simply can't partake in a relationship based on a fundamental principal I don't agree with."

Crystal smacked her lips and pressed her palms together at chest level. "What's the fundamental principal you're at odds with, darling?"

"Polygamy." Maggie's tongue tripped over the word.

"Ah, polygyny. Technically, that's the term you should be using. It's been practiced throughout history. In some parts of the world it still is, to great benefit of the people, especially where the male population is in decline."

Maggie looked at Paul, who was smiling with admiration in Crystal's direction. She released a dejected breath. "I don't care what you call it. It's not for me."

Crystal's tongue clucked as she moved closer to Paul and Katherine. "You'll have to excuse this beautiful spirit. As free-minded as I've raised her to be, she resists."

Gripping the travel amulet through her cotton shirt, Maggie dreamed of escape, but she didn't expect the piece of jewelry to do any more than give her someplace to put her hands other than yanking out the hair on her head.

"I'm sorry you wasted the trip, Paul." Maggie stepped between her mother and the unexpected guests. "Katherine, it was nice meeting you. I wish you both the sincerest blessings on your search for another wife, but please, stop considering me. I'm not an option."

Crystal patted Maggie on the back. "Maybe Maggie's not the soul you're searching for." She moved into the center of the circle. "Perhaps you'd consider me."

Maggie fainted.

*

The landing was bumpy, but the bumps in the air couldn't compare to the bump on Maggie's forehead. She reached with soft fingers and gently pressed the half-dollar-sized lump above her left eye. No stitches were required, but even after hours of ice, the wound still rose an inch off the surface of her skin. A bright purple line ran diagonally through the red circle where her head met the edge of a twelve-hundred-pound railroad tie table.

She snorted in pain and looked at the time on her phone. She could take more medicine in three hours. Until then, she'd remain as still as possible and breathe through the hurting.

"Whaddya do to your head?"

Maggie eased her gaze to the driver's bright green eyes reflected in the rearview mirror. "I fell against a table."

"Ouch." The large man named Bernie chuckled. His shoulders shook above the black leather seat of an expensive Lincoln town car.

Maggie knew Jordon represented baseball's best, but she never imagined him rich enough to employ a driver. At the airport she expected to ride in a taxi, not Lincoln's lap of luxury. Then again, maybe this was a car service Jordon paid on the side.

"Do you drive for Mr. Kemmons often?"

"Full-time in the off-season, part-time the rest of the year. He has players down here November through February. I get them where they're going."

Players. Plural. She was under the impression the house held one player, Carlos Nunez.

She sighed. What if there were more? A veritable dormitory of testosterone-drunk young men, who lived on alcohol and foul language while they scratched themselves in inappropriate places and left dirty laundry lying around. She couldn't work in conditions like that.

"How many people are staying at Jordon's house right now?"

Bernie laughed again. "One, but he's plenty."

Maggie's back straightened. "How so?"

"Carlos is a handful. He cries a lot. He never leaves the house, and he's got Jordon at the end of his rope. But I bet you already knew that."

Maggie didn't know that, and knowing didn't help foster a successful first meeting. From the moment she walked into Jordon's pristine house to the moment she caught sight of Carlos Nunez slumping on a hammock strung between two palm trees, she felt overwhelmed, defeated and far from home.

Tears flooded the young man's face when she introduced herself, and they continued to fall as she walked away. Jordon was lucky he lived in New York City. If he was in North Carolina, she would've dragged him to the end of the pier and pushed him off, despite the wrath of karma.

With the phone pressed to her ear and her gaze glued on Carlos's drooping back, Maggie bounced her head off the glass sliding door in frustration. The injured spot exploded with pain and she hollered to release the flow of energy at the precise moment that Jordon answered his phone.

"Dr. Collins, I presume. Let me guess. Another spider?" He

sounded unusually gruff, which may have had something to do with her yelling in his ear again.

"No. Sorry. I bumped my head, which is irrelevant." Maggie covered the wound with a soft palm and filled her nose with air. "What is relevant is that Carlos speaks Spanish."

"Of course he speaks Spanish. He's from the Dominican Republic."

"Didn't you think that was an important detail? I don't speak Spanish." Her head throbbed.

"He understands and speaks English."

"Nothing in there sounds remotely like English. I need a translator."

"Oh for God's sake, Maggie, are you really that incompetent?"

Maggie. Something swelled inside of her when he said her name. Other men said her name, sort of pushed it from their lips and lingered on the long E sound, like a whine. But not Jordon. He breathed her name. She thought he put the emphasis on the M, like the sound people made when something tasted particularly yummy. She wasn't sure, though. She wished he would say it again—for clarification.

"If you're gearing up to scream at me, please don't. This airport is a nightmare, and I can't be held responsible for my actions if one more thing goes wrong today."

Maggie watched Carlos slip off the hammock and walk down the sloping yard to the water's edge. "I don't know what to do if I can't communicate with him."

"Then consider yourself one hell of a high-priced babysitter."

Carlos jumped into the lake fully clothed.

Maggie screamed and dropped her phone.

Carlos's head never broke the surface as she rushed down the three-tiered deck to the spot where he plunged off the rock wall and into the gloomy lake. She stood on the same edge, eyes darting over the blackened sheet of glass.

"Mother Goddess, hear my prayer."

Maggie jumped into the water, too.

The chilly water stole her breath and burned her eyes, but still she managed to tangle a hand in the hood of Carlos's sweatshirt, yanking him to the surface where she could wrap an arm around his body.

Up ahead, the wooden pier sat lower to the water than the rock wall, and although he was conscious, he wasn't much help. Maggie blinked the lake from her eyes and figured her best chance of getting him out of the water without hurting either one of them was to swim with him to the pier and force him up the ladder.

With her arms locked underneath his armpits, she craned her head above the water and kicked like someone yelled, "Shark!"

Several exhausted minutes later, Maggie gripped the ladder as every muscle in her body shrieked. Despite the pain, she pushed and prodded until he climbed the metal steps and she dragged her beaten body onto the pier, where she collapsed—lungs burning and chest heaving—soaking wet on the planks, chilled to her weary core.

Shoving her arms and hands underneath her body for warmth, Maggie studied the man beside her. His left cheek rested against the pier like her right cheek did. His eyes hid behind earth-brown skin. Water dripped off the edge of his wide nose. And although he'd plunged into bottomless water fully clothed, prompting a chaotic rescue, he looked peaceful.

Her heart pounded against the timber.

"Carlos?" Maggie laid a hand on his wet cheek. "Let me help you."

He remained still, and she locked eyes on his shoulders, checking for movement. She rubbed his face and in a nervous panic, looked for his aura. Nothing. She didn't feel anything either. Maybe that was the projection. Emptiness.

Crystal preached emptiness as a euphoric state sans desire,

where a person could achieve true joy and happiness without attachment. Carlos's emptiness looked nothing like euphoria.

Maggie sucked a shaky breath and tried to break through again. "Listen. I don't know baseball. I'm not here to talk about baseball. I'm here to talk about you, but I don't speak Spanish. Wait, *si*...that's yes, right? Oh, and *hola*. I know that too. I'm sure there are other words that'll come to me, but not enough to carry on a conversation, and I want to talk to you, to learn why you're hurting."

He opened his eyes. Bright gold circles flanked by dripping black lashes stared at her through rapid blinks. She waited for him to speak, giving him as much time as he needed.

When his sharply angled lips made no movement, Maggie forged ahead. "Are you mad that I pulled you out?"

"No."

It was one word, but she wanted to cradle him to her chest in celebration. "Good, because I'd do it again. I save things. When I was little, my mother and I rescued a crow from the side of the road, and we nursed it back to health. He stunk and made too much noise. But when we released him in the canyon, and I watched him fly above the trees, my heart exploded." She patted Carlos's cheek. "I'm going to get you to fly again, and that's a promise."

The water trickling down his face wasn't from the lake, and she instinctively swiped at the tears. "Do you meditate?" She pushed off the scratchy wood and sat, pulling her knees to her chest.

He followed her with his eyes.

"Meditation is like prayer," she said, patting the pier. "Sit by me, and we can pray together."

He didn't move.

Maggie refused to be discouraged. She folded her legs into a pretzel with opposite ankles resting atop opposite inner thighs. Straightening her back, she dropped her shoulders and softened her forehead. Her tongue pressed loosely to the roof of her mouth. Her lips parted slightly, and her hands rested palm up on her knees. She let her gaze linger on the glossy water and distant trees before her lids slipped closed and her mind emptied in search of something strong enough to save them both.

CHAPTER THREE

Jordon didn't tread lightly. He preferred the opposition to see him coming and quake in their shoes. But the vision on his pier stopped him cold, and when he moved forward again, his feet barely touched the composite decking.

As he walked closer, Maggie came into clearer view. He saw the bumps of her spine stacked one on top of the other, perfectly perpendicular to the faded planks she sat upon. Her squared-off shoulders rounded at the edges, and he followed the long line of her arm to the barest glimpse of knee where an upturned hand rested. He swept his gaze back over her arm and shoulder to her graceful neck, supporting a head full of black velvet hair.

He tried to swallow, but struggled with the mindless motion.

When he was a few feet away, he saw her eyes were closed as she sat in a traditional pose for meditation. He didn't feel the least bit compelled to roll his eyes, which may have been a first. On the contrary, if he weren't dressed in a two-thousand-dollar Versace suit, he'd drop to the pier beside her and share the peace. For a moment, he wallowed in the emergence of foreign feelings, but then darkened when he thought about the chaos that would destroy his peace the minute Maggie opened her mouth.

He knew his words would come out rough—maybe even startle her—so he quieted as much as possible. "What the hell happened?"

Her eyes stayed closed as she brought her hands to her chest in prayer formation and mouthed something he couldn't understand. When she turned to face him, all he could see was a head wound the size of a golf ball above her brow.

The uneasy impulse to touch her forehead lifted his hand, but he shoved the wayward limb into a pocket instead. "Did you get that here?"

"No." She pulled the edges of her skirt over bare knees and unfurled to stand, moving like an over-sexed ballerina. When she stretched her arms into the air, her tank lifted over the milky skin of her flat belly.

Jordon adjusted an unwelcomed movement below his Louis Vuitton belt and blasted an exhale through his nose. "Are you going to tell me what happened here or do I have to guess?"

The gruffness returned, but by then he was too distracted to care. His gaze, having dropped to her chest, stuck on two dark, hard circles poking against her flimsy shirt.

He shrugged out of his jacket and stepped forward, pressing the silk lining to her back and yanking the peaked lapels over her breasts.

"I'm fine." She wiggled to shed the jacket.

"You're not fine. You're cold. Trust me. I can tell." He returned his hands to his pockets, feeling rather chivalrous.

Her brown eyes widened, and he realized how disproportionate they were to her long, lean face. Round and bright, they looked almost cartoonish. Once again, he thought of Betty Boop. But this time, his twisted brain took the thought a step further. Betty Boop—naked.

It had been a long day, long enough to turn classic children's television into porn. His face bunched with wrinkles of disgust.

"I'll wear it because it's painfully obvious you're as uncomfortable with the human body as you are with spirituality. But for my peace of mind, let me tell you…I could have this conversation completely naked and not think twice about it."

Jordon's peace of mind shattered. "I don't give a flying fuck what you are or aren't wearing. Just tell me what happened."

Maggie lifted her face to the early-November sun and filled her lungs so deeply a flood of fresh air landed in his gut. "Carlos jumped into the lake, and I pulled him out." Her voice reeked of calm, like she rescued sinking souls every day.

"You overreacted." Jordon knew the kid had issues, but suicidal thoughts weren't among them.

"No such thing when it comes to a client's safety," she huffed.

He tried to imagine the scene he'd missed. It didn't make sense. "Maybe he wanted to swim."

"In a hooded sweatshirt and construction boots?"

Jordon refused to believe Carlos was beyond fixing, but a familiar heaviness sat on his chest. He reached a hand to his heart and scratched at the discomfort, knowing it wasn't physical. His physician had proclaimed him healthy as an ox.

Maggie let the jacket slide off her shoulders, and handed it to him as she passed. "I'm going to check on him again, but you need to make arrangements for someone to stay with him fulltime, or he'll have to be admitted. He can't be left alone."

Jordon wasn't a PhD, but he knew a thing or two about the inner workings of men. First, physical health—as it related to appearance—was always more important than emotional health, at least in the circles he frequented. And second, only a man could feel certain sadness and basic lust near simultaneously.

Without much thought to her parting words, Jordon watched her walk away. Her bright skirt bounced against her backside. For narrow hips, they sure swung with enthusiasm.

A lump filled his throat right before a lump filled his pants.

"Maggie, don't you want to know why I'm here?" He let her believe he planned to stay in New York while she conducted her assessment. It was easier that way. As it was, he sensed her hesitation over being here hadn't waned.

She cut across the lower tier of the deck, running her hand along the rope railing. "I know why you're here, Mr. Kemmons. You're checking up on the flake you hired, because you doubted she could handle the job. Well you're right. Bravo," she called, emphasizing the words with a little hand clap. "Find someone else for the job. And…you can call me Dr. Collins."

Jordon would do nothing of the sort. He'd call her whatever he damn well wanted to call her. And at the moment, it was all he could do not to call her back.

*

Maggie wandered through the house, until she came across the room where Carlos was sleeping. Once again, she stayed by his side until she was positive he wasn't faking sleep to avoid talking, and then she dragged her suitcase to a bathroom in the main hall.

She changed out of her wet clothes and thought about the current situation. Carlos jumped in the lake. Jordon showed up after all. And Maggie hid in a bathroom, trying to decide how to deal with a confused twenty-year-old and a dark man who scared the living light out of her.

A strange sensation lingered in her chest ever since Jordon said her name on the pier, and her head hurt again. She leaned over the vanity to the mirror and studied the red bump on her forehead that turned blue at the edges. The rest of her head hurt, too, not only because of the localized pain from before.

Her stomach grumbled, and Maggie smoothed a palm over her belly. No wonder her head hurt. The last thing to cross her lips had been a stack of gluten-free crackers in Chicago's O'Hare Airport.

She'd been looking forward to a quiet evening of room service in order to build up enough emotional and mental strength to call Crystal for details about what ultimately happened with Paul. So much for quiet. Now Maggie had to haul her empty stomach and humungous headache out of this bathroom to face Jordon Kemmons.

Maggie emerged from the bathroom with a scowl on her face, but her misery didn't last long. Through windows and sky lights, the setting sun blanketed the house in a comforting orange glow.

After setting her suitcase in the foyer, she clicked her heels across the wood floors to a gourmet kitchen where a single light glowed above the Viking range, spilling onto marble counters and tiled backsplash. Her stomach rumbled again.

She could hardly be expected to have an intelligent conversation in her current state, so she fought feelings of overstepping her boundaries and reached for the handle of the stainless steel refrigerator, opening the door. Meat, milk, eggs and cheese. Two lone pieces of fruit sat on the top shelf next to a half-full jar of pickles and a two-liter bottle of Mountain Dew. She peeked into the vegetable crisper and crinkled her nose at wilted lettuce and carrots blackened with age. Without a better option, she closed her hand around the least offensive piece of fruit, a marked-up Granny Smith's apple.

After picking some bruises from the surface with her green-painted finger nails, Maggie rinsed the apple until it shined. She snatched a bottle of spring water from a smaller, glass-door refrigerator and headed in search of Jordon. When she didn't find him in the communal areas of the house, she suspected he was busy behind a closed door, hopefully securing her replacement.

Sparkling lake beckoned from enormous windows stretching the full width of the dining room and living room. It wasn't an ocean view, but the scene conjured similar feelings of peace and awe. She slid a glass door open and filled her lungs with crisp evening air, tinged with the soft scent of fish and grass, dirt and wood.

Her gaze fell to the spot where Carlos jumped, and a chill picked at her arms. Why did he do it? What was he trying to accomplish? Death? Attention?

"Will you be joining me for dinner?"

The apple dropped, splitting at her feet. Maggie looked to the broken fruit and then to the man sitting in the shadows. His large body rocked back in a patio chair, and his long legs crossed at the ankles, propping on the edge of a stone table. He'd traded the expensive suit for a pair of athletic shorts that gathered dangerously high on his powerful thighs. She glanced at his large hands resting on his flat stomach, atop a red T with a black swoosh stretching across his thick chest.

As Maggie bent for the apple, the talisman bounced against the inside of her shirt. *You can never have too much knowledge and understanding.* The ghost of Crystal's words carried on the wind. But Jordon wasn't the kind of man Maggie needed to know or understand. Every nerve ending warned her to stay away and yet the same intense curiosity and lust for life that pulled Crystal into chaos, tugged at Maggie.

"Did you hear me?"

She grabbed the apple and reminded herself to breathe. "Yes, I did, but I'm just going to eat this apple."

Jordon looked at the smashed fruit in her hands and a sort of smile touched his full lips. "Good luck with that."

The near-smile made her feel itchy and overheated. Why she felt that way begged for analysis, but she pushed the wayward thoughts from her mind in favor of a more appropriate topic. "I checked on Carlos. He was sleeping."

"Or pretending to sleep so he can ignore you." Jordon looked from her to the watery backyard.

Maggie watched him watch the water. Maybe he seemed softer because his eyes weren't challenging her or burning black as coal from this perspective.

She stepped toward the table. "As a mental health professional I'm obligated to intervene when a client is a risk to self or others."

Jordon's nose twitched but otherwise he remained the picture of calm. "Carlos is not at risk, unless you consider obsessively watching HGTV and reruns of *American Idol* harmful to one's health."

"He jumped into a lake fully clothed, and he stayed underwater long enough for me to worry. Now, in the end he climbed the ladder on his own, so there's ambiguity there, but there's also enough desperation in the act to make me take notice. He needs constant supervision until we know for sure."

"You can take one of the guest rooms. I'll have my secretary cancel your hotel reservation."

The words wrapped like a noose around her neck and blocked the air to her lungs.

"What?" Jordon badgered. "I hardly think that's asking too much. Besides, you'll be compensated."

No amount of money in the world could calm her nerves over staying under the same roof as a client. "Can't his family stay with him?"

The smooth skin around Jordon's wide mouth wrinkled. "He refuses to see them. I offered to fly him home or fly them here. His post-season performance was atrocious, and he's embarrassed. Baseball's a big deal where he's from."

"I'm not so sure this is about baseball. What about financial or personal problems?"

"If Carlos's money was a mess, I'd know. Financial management is serious business to my firm."

"What about personal life?"

"No idea. He doesn't talk to me about his private life—never has. The more I push, the more he clams up."

Maggie smiled. She couldn't help the expression. People amazed her. They missed the "big picture" all the time. "Carlos is intimidated by you."

Jordon slid his hands over his stomach to cup his elbows and set his square chin in defiance. "That's ridiculous."

"News flash, Mr. Kemmons; you're scary. Your body language reveals arrogance and unyielding thought. Physically, you're an imposing man. You rarely smile. You rarely laugh. And you seem to judge people based on outdated, egotistical assumptions. It makes sense a troubled young man would display silence in the face of your pushing."

"Is that so?" He snapped forward, and the chair slapped against his back as his elbows shook the table.

Surprisingly, Maggie didn't flinch. She was too busy studying him, noticing how his chin-to-hand posture mimicked hers and his eye contact intensified. "Yes. It is. Take your sudden movement, for instance. You were testing me—subconsciously maybe, but definitely testing me—to see how much power you held over my reaction. You like power, and I bet this demeanor helps you close deals, but it wreaks havoc on your personal life. Let me ask you this, did it bother you that I didn't give you any power—that I didn't flinch?"

His eyes darkened.

She sat back against the cushioned chair, crossing one leg over the other and balancing her elbows on the armrests with her hands folded in front of her. "Another example would be your outdated and egotistical notion of me."

"You?" Jordon sat back and assumed Maggie's relaxed posture, legs crossed and hands folded.

"Me. Because I'm not like the people in your world, you think I'm…flaky." She raised a finger when his lips twitched. "And despite the frustration my flakiness seems to cause you, you're curious about me and struggling with how to feed that curiosity." The minute he ran the tip of his tongue over his rounded bottom lip, she wished she'd picked less suggestive words.

He raised a thick brow and licked again. "Are you getting all of this from a crystal ball?"

"Hardly that fantastical. It's non-verbal communication, and you're mirroring me."

"What?" He slammed his brows together as soon as he noticed their similar postures.

Squeezing his arms across his chest, Jordon kicked his feet onto the table. "That's dime store psychology, and I'm paying for more than that, Dr. Collins." He bit into the title and glowered at the falling darkness behind her.

Maggie's stomach churned, and she knew it wasn't because of hunger. Stirring his anger accomplished a not-so-subtle reminder that intellectual flirting came with a hefty price tag, and she couldn't spend an ounce of the money she hoped to earn. An independent future hinged on Carlos's recovery.

"I don't think Carlos wants to die. I think it was an experiment of sorts with a little attention-seeking mixed in. Maybe he was testing me."

Jordon looked at her again and the wrinkles around his mouth and eyes disappeared.

"I mean obviously if I thought he was at risk, I would've called 911." She lifted her eyes to the sky and shook her head before leveling her gaze on Jordon. "But I also know that would cause a stir, and you want to keep things hushed. Bottom line is, I can stick around and give him some emergency therapy, but he needs twenty-four-hour supervision, too."

"I leave for Venezuela tomorrow."

She was running out of options. "Can Bernie stay with him?"

"I don't want Bernie to stay with him. I want you. I hired you."

"You hired me for a consultation and virtual therapy, not for residential treatment in your home."

"The two-month salary for a therapist on my payroll is thirty-two thousand dollars. Would you stay for that kind of money, Dr. Collins?"

Maggie swallowed the urge to take the money and worry about the consequence later.

"No? Not enough," he mused. "How about this? Carlos is eight miles per hour off on his fastball. I'll throw in two grand for each mile per hour increase, and if you get him over the one hundred-mile-per-hour mark, I'll pay a ten-thousand-dollar bonus."

He was clearly a man who knew the power of paper.

"You won't find a more lucrative deal," he added with a sly smile.

"I have other clients, Mr. Kemmons."

"I have internet connections, Dr. Collins."

"I didn't pack enough clothes."

"I have laundry facilities, and Lake Norman has stores. I also have a postal address, should you want items from home shipped to you."

"I'm not comfortable spending time alone with him."

"He's a broken kid, not a serial killer. Besides, I'll be back as much as I can. Bernie will be nearby, should you need help. Speaking of the devil..."

The sliding door opened, and Bernie walked toward them with a brown bag in each hand. "Boss Man. Dr. Collins."

Jordon grabbed a bag from Bernie with a weak curve to his lips, like he wanted to smile but didn't know how. He dug into the bag and pushed a tray of sushi toward her.

"No, thank you. Bernie can have mine. I'll go see if Carlos is awake."

Bernie swatted a humongous hand in front of him. "My dinner's in the car. I'm headed home...but I can poke my head in on Carlos before I go. If he's up, I'll let you know." He pounded the knuckles of his fist against Jordon's knuckles and nodded at Maggie. "You kids be good now."

Through the wall of windows, she watched him walk across the great room and up the stairs. "He should've stayed and eaten with you instead of eating alone."

Jordon looked up from his chopsticks, gripping a California roll covered in soy sauce and wasabi. He chewed as he studied her, his gaze drifting from her eyes to her lips.

The scrutiny shouldn't bother Maggie. Crystal taught her letting someone look their fill was the greatest gift of clarity you could give. But if truth lurked behind the eyes, Maggie worried what Jordon might see.

He finished chewing, and set the chopsticks aside. "Did it ever dawn on you that you don't know everything about everybody?"

"I never said that I do know everything." She pulled on a silver hoop dangling from her ear.

"Bernie is married with two little girls. He would much rather eat with them than with a scary ogre like me."

"Oh."

"Exactly." Jordon popped another California roll into his mouth. "Eat."

"I'm sorry. I can't."

He reached across the table and pulled the top off the plastic plate. "It's vegetarian. Cross my heart. I didn't sneak an ounce of caviar in there." The chopsticks that he pulled from his mouth mere seconds ago danced millimeters above her food. "See? You've got avocado, sprouts, cucumber. That looks like dill pickle." He pinched a roll between the sticks and tossed it into his mouth. "I'll be damned. That's good."

She expected him to be damned…but he ordered her vegetarian sushi. Now she wasn't sure. "Did I tell you I was vegetarian?"

"No. I listen. It's an occupational hazard. I figured if you won't kill a spider, you certainly won't eat fish eggs. Have Bernie take you to the store tomorrow or give him a list. Harris Teeter isn't far, and they have a big selection of health foods."

Maggie scratched at a hot spot of skin above her breast. Just because he thought to feed her appropriately didn't make him any less lethal to her enlightenment. Distance. Detachment. She had a job to do.

Stuffing her mouth with a sushi roll, Maggie hoped to swallow the emotions too.

"What's the story behind the bump on your head?" His gaze lingered on the wound she was increasingly able to forget.

"I fell."

"Must've fallen pretty hard."

"I fainted and hit the end of a table. The ER doctor was

surprised I didn't have a concussion." She tapped the top of her skull. "I'm hardheaded."

"Another spider?"

"No." She wished. "I'm not always weird about spiders. That one seemed aggressive, and the night already wasn't going my way, so I overreacted."

"Did you talk to him?"

She rolled her eyes. "Yes. I did. I know you think that's strange, but I talked to him as I shooed him out and stuffed a rug under the crack so he couldn't return."

"And did he talk back?"

"Ha Ha." She filled her mouth again and hummed while she chewed. She hadn't realized how hungry she was until the rice mixed with cold vegetable filling and the spicy smell of wasabi burned the lining of her nose.

"What made you faint?" Jordon hadn't taken his eyes off of her since Bernie left.

Despite the cool, night air, a hot tingle walked along her skin. "It's a long story."

"We have all night."

She felt sweaty; itchy, too. He stared at her like he expected the pressure from his eyes to force the story from her lips. And like that, his intense stare dropped to her mouth.

Maggie thought back to the pier and his reaction to her nipples showing through her top. She wondered if his gaze would travel down.

Jordon looked to the horizon instead.

She wasn't surprised. She wasn't blessed with a milk factory. Her small breasts didn't bother her, and she had yet to hear a lover complain. Still, she imagined a man like Jordon wanted more than his house and bank account to be super-sized. For some reason, that bothered her. And the fact that it bothered her bothered her, because it didn't matter. She didn't want him to be attracted to her. She wasn't attracted to him.

Maggie choked on a sliver of rice wrapped in denial.

"You're not going to tell me, are you? You don't want to be embarrassed." He finished chewing his last California roll and pushed away from the table.

"Embarrassment is fleeting, like all emotion." She watched him walk to the outdoor kitchen and bend over a lower cabinet. *Like lust.* Her eyes lingered a bit too long on the muscle stretching the fabric. *Lust is definitely a fleeting emotion.*

When the heat in her cheeks didn't fade like she expected, she poked her face with chopsticks.

"Beer? Wine? I have chardonnay and pinot grigio out here. If you want red, I'll have to go inside."

"Water."

He straightened and turned dark eyes on her. "No animal died to make this beer." He held a thin can. "I'm not even sure it's beer. It's damn close to water."

"Then why do you drink it?"

"I'm on the road a lot, and I eat like hell. I cut calories when I can." His eyes narrowed. "Water?" He dangled a second can in front of her. "Come on. One drink. It's a beautiful night. Despite what you say, I think we're building a friendship, *Maggie.* You're just afraid to admit it."

"I'm not afraid of anything." Okay, so that was a blatant lie.

Guilt picked at her conscience. In Maggie's experience, guilt wasn't a fleeting emotion, but she suspected living with a little guilt was better than letting Jordon Kemmons penetrate her competent exterior. Maggie crossed her arms, lifted her chin and attempted to look tough.

Jordon wasn't buying. He scoffed in her direction. "You're afraid of spiders. I also think you're afraid you'll drink this beer, think I'm not a horrible person and spill your guts." He cleared something from his throat. "Or you'll get tipsy and belly dance…

like you did in New York."

He sat, and Maggie watched emotion flicker across his face. She was usually good at naming reactions, but that brief second of feeling passed across his tanned skin before she could interpret. Then again, maybe she was distracted by the itch that started in her breast and settled deep in her belly.

She remembered the dance, an innocent send-off for a favorite professor. But by the look of Jordon's reddened face, his interpretation of the act was much less innocent. The idea grew the itch. Touching a hand to her stomach, she sought relief by digging her fingernails into the flesh. The worthless action stirred her discomfort.

"Mr. Kemmons, you're goading me, and I imagine you do something similar when you're negotiating a contract where the other party is stonewalling."

He shrugged and dragged a hand across his mouth. "I neither confirm nor deny the accusation. My negotiation tactics are my trade secrets." He winked. "You're not the only one with secrets."

The itch clawed up Maggie's chest and created a blazing trail over her face. Embarrassment? Maybe. With a little misguided desire thrown in too.

She waited for the emotions to pass, breathing in through her nose and out through her mouth. She would've done fine settling her feelings had he not been staring at her reddened face with a curve to his lips that looked dangerously close to a smile.

Maggie huffed. "Oh, for crying out loud, it's not a secret. I have hyperventilation syndrome. My breathing gets whacky when I'm overly stressed, and if I don't get a handle on it, I pass out."

"What made you overly stressed?"

"A man I dated showed up at my house with his wife." That sounded horrible. Maggie held up both hands. "It was one date, and I didn't know he was married. He told me he was a polygamist as soon as we sat down to eat."

Jordon's eyes wiggled, and her itch abated. He pressed his thick lashes together over and over again, and she thought maybe he struggled with contact lenses, but then his mouth split open and his lips curled over the straightest line of snow white teeth. He tossed back his head to the sky and laughed with such rich cadence, it resonated in her soul.

Maggie laughed, too. "If you think that's funny, wait. I didn't faint until my mother showed interest in Paul's polygamist proposal."

Jordon stopped laughing and dropped his chin to his chest. His smile disappeared. "Your mother is interested in a polygamous relationship with a man you dated?"

Well, when he put it like that…

She shook her head at the foolishness. There were times when an open-minded, alternative life felt like living inside a big fat joke. "I dated Paul once. It's not like we were serious. Not that that makes my mother's interest any less awkward." She pressed a finger into her temple and rubbed. "I can't imagine she's serious. I hope not. I passed out, went to the ER, and the evening was foggy from there. The next thing I clearly remember, a taxi was beeping in the driveway, and Crystal was MIA."

He took a drink from the silver can. "You call your mother by her first name?"

"I do. She doesn't like labels." Maggie followed his hand as he brushed a few stray drops from his bottom lip. The itch returned. "Anyhow…I haven't talked to her since. She's not answering her phone. Maybe she's married and on her honeymoon with her new husband and sister wife."

Maggie forced a laugh. She didn't believe it. At least she didn't want to believe it. Still, Crystal did as Crystal pleased, as long as the stars were aligned. Maggie raised her face to heaven.

Jordon slid his beer across the table. "You need this more than I do."

She actually contemplated a sip. Instead, she smiled and pushed the itch deeper into her gut while she stuffed empty sushi containers into paper bags.

"Thanks, but you can keep your beer." She set the can in front of him. "Numbing emotions doesn't solve anything."

Raising the beer to his mouth, Jordon stared at her while he drained the can. "Then let me show you to your room."

The itch covered her entire body.

"You're assuming I'm staying, Mr. Kemmons."

"You're still here, aren't you?"

Maggie sucked a steady stream of cool air into her nose. "Fine. I'll stay until Carlos is cleared to be alone or until you find a suitable replacement, whichever comes first."

Jordon stood and held out his hand.

She waved him off. "I want those terms in writing."

He chuckled. "Of course. You can take the guest room across from Carlos's room. There's a lock on the door...in case you get scared."

Maggie flashed a snotty smile. "I'm not scared of anything, Mr. Kemmons." *Not even you*, she gulped.

"Good night...Maggie."

He definitely lingered on the M.

CHAPTER FOUR

A black spider dangled from the ceiling above Maggie's guest suite bed. His lithe body bounced a few feet from her face, and she froze with fear.

I'm not afraid. I'm not afraid. The words ran through her mind like a mantra.

But she was afraid. Her heart pounded in her throat and perspiration dripped off her forehead. She drew a quivering breath, preparing to speak, but the spider plummeted, and she rolled out of bed, hitting the hardwood floor.

Strange. She remembered a carpeted floor. With one eye on her surroundings and the other hunting for the spider, Maggie zipped backward and slammed against a pair of strong legs. She scurried around on all fours to see Paul and Katherine standing over her.

You're misjudging me. Can't you see who I am? Their lips didn't move.

She dropped her head, and the spider appeared beside her right hand.

Save me.

Maggie bolted upright in bed. She raised a hand to her pulsing chest and steadied her breathing. Sunlight lined the cracks of window blinds, and she realized she'd slept late. Morning dreams were always the most powerful, and this one perplexed her. Reaching to the bedside table, she grabbed her phone, hoping Crystal could interpret the dream before Maggie took another stab at interpreting Carlos.

Thirty minutes later, a freshly showered Maggie sulked. Carlos was awake, but he wouldn't get out of bed, and Crystal wouldn't answer the phone. Jordon left for the airport before Maggie woke, leaving her alone, ornery and homesick.

Spreading a blanket from the upstairs linen closet across the lowest tier of decking, she sat and crossed her legs, resting her hands on her knees. She didn't chant this time. Instead, she focused on her breathing and imagined her spine stretching to the cloudless sky. She counted ten deep breaths and raised her arms over her head, sweeping them down again, feeling the morning air dance across her skin.

After a few more sweeps with her arms, she rolled onto all fours and tilted her tail bone before she curled her spine, repeating the motion over and over again with her eyes soft and focused on the rippling water. When she'd completed the entire sequence of postures, she sat with the stillness until she opened herself to enough peace and positive light to continue with the day. Folding the blanket, she padded her bare feet into the house.

Carlos sat on the couch, watching newlyweds choose between three Cape Cod-style homes. House Number Three had an in-ground swimming pool and sloping backyard.

"Pretty," Maggie said as she draped the blanket over the back of the couch. "But I bet they don't pick that one. They seem too traditional. She'll be pregnant within the year, and the pool and yard aren't child-friendly." She didn't expect him to reply. She was simply tired of talking to herself.

"One and Two are far from work. He goes downtown. They have one car. He wants to bike...or walk." Carlos spoke perfect English with a melodic accent.

Maggie grabbed the couch and held her breath.

"See. They picked Three," Carlos muttered.

She stole a glance at him. He harbored great sadness in the lines of his face. "You were right. Good call." She didn't want to push. Eventually they would talk about what happened in the lake, but not now. Now she needed to establish trust, let him know she was his ally.

Maggie walked to the kitchen. "Are you hungry? Can I make you lunch?"

"No."

Since she hadn't called Bernie to arrange a trip to the supermarket, the only remaining piece of fruit was a wrinkled peach—at least she thought it was a peach. She closed the refrigerator door and started digging through the cupboards.

"Do you do yoga every day?"

Maggie closed the cupboard door and turned. Carlos stood on the other side of the kitchen island, leaning over the gritty Hibachi grill, studying her with flat eyes.

"I try to. It's good to have a routine. Routines help even out the high and low points of a day." She smiled. "You're welcome to join me."

He seemed to think about her offer, and she wondered if his face was always round or if the crying made it extra puffy.

"Paris. I saw this one." Carlos looked at the giant flat screen hanging above the fire place. "They pick the place in Le Marais."

Maggie didn't know whether to laugh, cry or drop to her knees and thank the Universal Good. For whatever reason, Carlos was talking, and she wanted to keep it that way. "I love Paris. Would it be okay if I watched with you, or did you have something else to do?"

He bit into his wheat-colored bottom lip, contemplating again. "We can watch."

When he shuffled off, Maggie followed.

By evening, her head throbbed and her stomach cramped, but she'd spent almost seven hours with Carlos. They learned that real deals lurked south of Decatur, Georgia, buying property in the Italian countryside meant more than likely some part of your ancient home would be falling down, and Kelly Clarkson didn't receive enough screen time early on in Season One of *American Idol*.

There were other lessons in there too, like through observation, Maggie discovered Carlos had a tattoo of a crucifix on his right bicep. The faded, blue artwork appeared when he raised his arm to point at the crystal blue waters of Fiji. "Like home."

He didn't say another word about his island nation, and Maggie refused to push. At the moment, she didn't care if he spoke another word all night. Crystal's voice was the one she wanted to hear.

The woman still wasn't answering the phone or returning Maggie's messages. Between the hunger and the worry and the realization that the kitchen harbored more animal products than a zoo, Maggie felt defeated and unable to fully enjoy the strides she'd made with Carlos.

Visions of vegetarian Pad Thai danced in her head.

"Special delivery." Bernie carried two arms full of plastic grocery bags into the kitchen where he deposited them onto the counter.

Maggie jumped to her feet. The lack of food in her stomach and the sudden movement caused a splotchy spinning in her head. "What is this?"

"You gotta eat, Dr. Collins. Why didn't you call me?"

"I didn't want to bother you." That, and she didn't want her focus to leave Carlos.

"It's my job. You gotta let me earn my living," he said with a smile.

Maggie dipped into the nearest bag. Fresh apples, crisp lettuce, firm red and green peppers. Her mouth watered.

She pulled another bag toward her. Tofu, almonds, walnuts, cashews. She nearly exploded from an overabundance of joy.

With Bernie's help, she put away six bags filled with foods from apples to zucchinis. When she'd stacked the last can of legumes on a shelf, she closed the cupboard door and hugged the large man with all her might.

His laughter bounced her body. "What's this for?"

"Thank you."

He was still laughing when she pulled away and peeled back the plastic top on the almonds. She filled her hand and popped the nuts, one after the other, into her hungry mouth. "Soy milk too! I'm amazed. How are you such a vegetarian food expert?"

"Boss Man called to see if you called me. When I said no, he emailed me a list. You owe him that hug."

The words painted an image in her head, and a flame shot between her breasts, curling around her throat. She shuddered and popped another almond into her mouth. "I'm forever grateful, Bernie. What do I owe you?"

He balked and stuffed his hands in his pocket to jingle his keys. "Boss Man pays for everything. I'm just the driver. And right now, I gotta drive some chocolate chips to my girls. You take care, Dr. Collins, and you call me when you need something. You hear? You too, Carlos."

Bernie craned his thick neck toward the living room, and Maggie was surprised to see Carlos wave. Maybe things weren't so bad after all. Maybe Carlos was more stable than she thought.

If only she could say the same thing about her mother. Thousands of miles stretched out between them, and there was still no peace to be found.

Once Maggie's belly was full and her head was clear, she tried calling Crystal again.

"Blessings." Crystal answered the phone with her usual sing-song greeting.

Maggie skipped the sigh of relief. "I wish you would get a cell phone."

Folding her long legs underneath her, Maggie rested her left elbow on the arm of the chair Jordon filled the night before. She scanned the twinkling lights around the perimeter of the lake. Most of the glows came from distant houses, but an occasional moving light accompanied by a low rumbling signaled a boat.

"Magpie, cellular telephones rob us of privacy and peace. Besides, they cause cancer." Her tsk-tsks echoed over the line. "The older you get, the more you embrace the physical world. It should be the other way around. Let go of your attachments."

She was trying, but it wasn't working. Maggie thought of the refrigerator hidden behind plain cabinetry to her left. Chardonnay sounded good, but under the circumstances she worried she'd drink the whole bottle.

And she needed to be sober for this conversation.

"Are you attached to Paul and Katherine?" Maggie nibbled on the end of her nail and followed a blowing leaf as it tumbled across the deck through a path of light from the living room.

"That's not the kind of attachment I'm talking about, and you know it. Your ideology is straying from the universal, and I'm worried. As far as Paul goes, he's a lovely man."

"He's also a married man who's attached to a woman who doesn't speak. That doesn't strike you as odd?"

"Darling, she's submitting to his will. You and I may not understand that, but it's her reality and where she finds comfort."

Maggie's shoulders rose sharply, and her chest stung with cold night air. Crystal was right. Who was Maggie to judge? And yet it would be easier not to judge if her mother wasn't potentially mixed up in this. "Aren't you happy with your life the way it is? You don't need them."

"I wouldn't restrict myself the opportunity to know any soul unless that soul was void of light. I'm happy with life because I'm detached, Magpie. My worldly goods are minimal. I love freely and without fear of loss. It's taken me many years to get to this stage in my enlightenment, and I have no intention of losing ground."

The words were meant to reassure, but as Maggie closed her eyes and listened to her mother rambling about the benefits of detachment, she doubted more than she ever had. This was her life of extremes. One moment Maggie was a competent professional, helping challenged clients settle into mainstream society, the next she was deciphering her mother's teachings, a mix of the world's greatest religions, peppered with bizarre, lesser-known spiritual practices. Crystal warped the Buddhist practice of detachment into something Maggie had difficulty understanding. To Crystal, loving freely meant walking away on a whim, even from her daughter. Where Maggie thought sex complicated things, Crystal disagreed, saying physical relationships enhanced both the life and soul experiences. Maggie couldn't figure out how to benefit from those enhancements without becoming attached.

"It's about giving." Crystal had said, when Maggie was only eight. A naked man was playing an acoustic guitar in Crystal's bedroom, and Maggie remembered feeling scared and confused. Later on and over the years, Crystal restated her position a million times. "Sex is the ultimate act of giving. The minute you make it about receiving, you risk desire and attachment too great to overcome."

While other mothers preached about teen pregnancies and STDs, Maggie's mother preached about having sex without expecting anything in return. Was it any wonder Maggie was so confused?

Believing wholeheartedly in the Law of Attraction, Maggie always thought the time she spent worried about saving wayward souls attracted more souls in need, but the more she thought about it, the more she wondered if Jordon's impression of her wasn't right. Maybe she was…flaky. In that case, it would make sense for her to attract other…flakes.

"That's why Paul's offer is attractive."

Maggie's wandering mind rocketed to attention. "What offer?"

"Sorry, Magpie. My company has arrived. Love and light, darling."

The line clicked, and no matter how hard Maggie concentrated on breathing, the panic rose. What was Paul's offer? She should've paid closer attention. Dancing her fingers over the touch screen, she hoped and prayed, but Crystal never answered.

Hours later Maggie was awakened by a spider crawling noisily across her sea grass headboard. The arachnid inched toward her face. She tried to lift her head, but she stuck to the pillow, knowing if she didn't move, the spider would reach her, touch her, and bite her, sucking the life out of her petrified body.

Save me.

Maggie tried to lift her head again, and a pain shot through her neck.

Crystal appeared on the ceiling. *Magpie, detach.*

"I'm trying to," Maggie yelled, yanking her head off the pillow and snapping to a sitting position. This time, she held both hands to her pounding chest, worrying that she may have scared Carlos with the outburst.

Maggie didn't want to worry about her mother anymore, but she didn't know how to stop. She reached for her phone with trembling hands. If Crystal was unreachable, Maggie knew someone with critical information about her mother who wouldn't be.

"Hello? Maggie?" Paul sounded sleepy and disoriented.

Breathing in Jordon's air must have changed some of her cosmic makeup, because until now she did pay attention to clocks and time zones. She flinched, imagining eight little children sleeping in the same house and his docile wife curled at his side. She would've hung up if Caller ID hadn't already blown her cover.

"Paul, I'm sorry to bother you this late, but…I need to know what's going on with my mother."

"What do you mean? Is she okay?"

"That's my question exactly. I know this is going to sound crazy, but so be it. Please don't marry my mother." Foolishness burned the lining of her mouth.

"I'm not marrying your mother, Maggie."

Now she felt guilty on top of the foolishness. Sure the guy on the other end was a polygamist, an anomaly to most of the world, and yet she was the one calling a near-stranger in the middle of the night with an outlandish request.

"Crystal is far too old for anything other than a matriarchal position in the family, and Katherine isn't quite sure she's ready to be usurped in that way."

Isn't quite sure? His ambiguous words validated Maggie's fear. "If Katherine decides she's okay with being usurped, what then? Will you marry her then? This is my mother we're talking about. She's easily trusting and entirely too susceptible. I've been having dreams, and you're both in them, and you need me to save you. I'm trying, Paul. I am. Please leave her alone."

"Maggie, you're overreacting. Your mother is a beautiful visionary, and she's capable of making adult decisions."

She wished she could believe that, but past experience proved him wrong. "My mother is complicated, and I'm tired of worrying about what's next and if what's next is going to hurt her beyond repair."

"How would sharing a life with us hurt her?"

"What you call sharing, some people would call twisted oppression, male domination, and archaic, outdated, misguided religious doctrine." Maggie gasped. She couldn't believe she strung together so many negative labels. She sounded intolerant, just like Jordon. The man was thousands of miles away, but his negativity still influenced her.

She needed to get a grip. She needed to prioritize: save Carlos from himself, save Crystal from Paul, and save Maggie from this slippery slope.

CHAPTER FIVE

Maggie stared at a waist-high pile of dirty clothes in the middle of Carlos's bathroom. "Are you kidding me?" she asked.

"I don't know how to do it." He extended his lanky arms to shoulder height and shrugged. "I don't know where to send it."

"You could've asked Bernie." Maggie bit back a snicker as she scanned the only clothing on his skinny body, a thigh-strangling girdle Carlos called 'sliding shorts.' Maggie didn't know what sliding shorts were, but they didn't look comfortable. "They're cutting off your circulation."

"I don't think they're mine. They're too small."

She laughed and kicked an empty wicker basket toward him. "It'll take a couple trips, but I want you to carry this all downstairs and dump it into a pile in front of the washing machine. Then I'll teach you how to sort it. Sound like a plan?"

He nodded and filled the basket as his sliding pants strangled his thighs. There had to be something else he could wear. Even a blanket or towel wrapped around his waist would be more comfortable.

A solution popped into Maggie's head as she reached for a towel on a nearby rack. "I'm going to snoop through Jordon's things. I bet he has something you can wear."

Carlos reared his head and widened his eyes.

"What? Under the circumstances I hardly think he'd care." The look on Carlos's face gave Maggie second thoughts. "Do you think he'd care?"

Carlos filled his arms with more dirty clothes. "Maybe. He's..."

"Scary?" She meant to finish the sentence in her head, but she blurted the word instead.

"I was going to say private."

She squatted beside him, careful not to breathe too deeply in the direction of the pile. "I shouldn't have said that. Jordon is intense. That's all."

"*Sí.*" Carlos stood and hoisted the full basket to his waist. The heaping load in his arms didn't put a dent in the pile on the floor.

Maggie followed him to the loft and down the stairs, hoping her slip of the tongue wouldn't negatively influence Carlos where Jordon was concerned. The last thing she wanted to do was come between a player and his agent.

"Jordon had Bernie bring me all those groceries," she said, hoping to neutralize the conversation. "That was nice. Don't you think?"

"*Sí.*" Carlos turned and smiled. "He said you're welcome."

Over the last few days, she'd seen more and more cracks in Carlos's sadness. He was even up to eating twice a day, but after that comment, she wasn't interested in applauding his progress. Jordon had some explaining to do.

"You talk to Jordon?" she asked, trying not to sound like the injured party.

"Every night."

This was news to Maggie, who left three messages for Jordon. The first consisted of a 'thank you' for the groceries. The second revolved around Carlos's progress, and the third was to inform him that she sent the exterminator packing.

"Great. Well, he won't return my calls. I'm happy to know he checks in with you at least." So much for coming between a player and agent.

Carlos nodded and continued to the laundry room while Maggie stood in the same spot. Any friendly feelings she harbored for Jordon melted under the heat of this new information. Why was he ignoring her?

Oh, she could imagine what he thought of her last message. She recalled her exact words: "The insects you're murdering have received a stay of execution for the duration of my assignment. If that isn't acceptable to you, find someone to take my place." Par for the course when dealing with a *flake*.

She marched across the hardwoods and threw open the door to the master suite. Her feet sunk into snow-white carpeting and her breath caught at the lake view from floor-to-ceiling windows. A private deck and two loungers beckoned on the other side of glass. No curtains or blinds obstructed the scene, just water as far as the eyes could see.

She walked deeper into the room and admired the huge wrought iron bed with plump ebony linens. Matching black lacquered nightstands held short stacks of books and accent lamps topped with dark-as-night shades. She ran her finger tips over the cover of a Hank Aaron biography before she spun around in search of a dresser.

In the corner of the room, black leather club chairs shared a wrought iron coffee table and a flat screen hung above a low bureau. She crossed to the sitting area and tugged on the single drawer. Remote controls. Unused cell phones. Cords and... condoms. A couple blue packets escaped the open box.

Maggie gulped air, hoping to stomp the conflicting emotions pinching her lungs. Of course he had condoms. He was an attractive man. A little too dark for her taste, but lots of women would...she slammed the drawer shut and stared at the big bed. Lots of women would climb into bed with Jordan.

Her skin heated as the images entered her brain with rapid-fire precision. His face gone soft. His body gone hard. And the woman who inspired his magical transformation.

She slapped her cheek—twice—because the woman in the images was her.

Pounding her chest to restart her heart, Maggie focused on her mission: clothes for Carlos. She held her breath and walked by the bed, running a finger along the silky duvet. When she'd safely passed, she reached for a doorknob in the hopes of finding a closet. Instead, she scanned miles of black granite, covering the floors and running up the walls of a shower bigger than her bedroom at home.

Flecks of silver danced along the polished surfaces. The double sinks shone black with chrome fixtures, and the jetted tub seduced like a tar pit. Maggie swallowed hard.

This was where the devil came to play.

More unwelcomed images of Jordon filled her head. Him, standing in the shower...with her. The air in her nose and throat thickened like cement.

"Can I help you?"

She spun until her eyes locked on the jagged face behind the rough voice. "What are you doing here?"

"*This* is my bathroom. What are *you* doing here?"

He was surrounded by black, but Maggie's shaky vision couldn't tell if the color was the result of a negative aura or the wall of granite. She blinked fast and often, trying to see, trying to think.

His smoky running shoes, black jeans and fitted gray windbreaker blended with the dark stone. "You scared me." Could he hear her heart pounding? "I'm looking for clothes for Carlos."

He narrowed crow-like eyes. "Why would his clothes be in my room? And why would Carlos need your help getting dressed?"

The negative energy radiating from Jordon's core permeated her shield of light, and a rush of dark power coursed through her veins. "What are you insinuating?" She wrapped her arms around her breasts.

"Don't answer my question with a question." He folded his arms across his chest too.

"The poor kid doesn't know how to do laundry. If you weren't so intimidating, he would've asked for help. But you are who you are, so he's dressed in an uncomfortable piece of baseball equipment, and I'm trying to help." She blasted by him, striking him with a flailing arm.

Jordon was quicker than she anticipated, and he grabbed her trailing wrist, bringing her to a halt. "Why didn't you say that in the first place?"

"What, and miss you insulting me by insinuating I'm sleeping with a client?"

"It crossed my mind."

If he was trying to make her feel better, he failed. She ripped her wrist from his hand and gripped her amulet through the pale yellow fabric of an empire-waist Henley. His eyes followed, flashing back and forth over her breasts. Her stomach dipped. The deep breaths she struggled for didn't put a dent in her rising anger. "You're evil."

His cheek twitched. "Why? Because I think it's possible an attractive woman who obviously doesn't own a bra has the capability to bed a professional athlete?"

She'd never hit another person, but she no longer trusted her inner belief system to keep her from doing harm. Distance was the only thing that could save her soul. She was tired of his negativity, tired of being affected by it even when he wasn't here, and tired of the sight of him stirring a primal ache in her core.

He thought she was attractive. Big deal. He also thought she was a promiscuous, unprofessional flake. She might be in the midst of a delayed quarter-life crises, but she was none of the things Jordon thought she was.

Maggie fled the wicked room and came face to face with a sad-eyed Carlos. He had an orange bottle of detergent in hand and the face of a child caught in the middle of a nasty divorce.

She released her grip on the amulet, and something sensible surged. "Let's teach you how to do laundry." Her voice was a little too high, like a deranged preschool teacher, but it did the trick, and Carlos followed her to the laundry room.

He didn't speak while they sorted the darks from the lights. When everything piled with like colors, Maggie nodded. "We'll do this load first. Go ahead and fill the machine."

She watched as he lined the drum of the washer with a rainbow of clothes. When he'd finished, she handed him the detergent bottle. "Fill the cap to the top line." His hands shook, and she couldn't help but smile. "Now dump it." He hesitated. "Go ahead. Dump it all around or all in one spot. It doesn't matter. Good. Close the lid, and start the machine."

She showed him which buttons to press and which dials to turn, and when the machine started filling with water, he looked besotted.

"You can show me that one, too?" He pointed to the dryer.

"When the washing machine stops. Until then, maybe you should hang out in your room where you'll be more comfortable."

"Or you can change into these." Jordon loomed in the doorway, blocking the exit.

Carlos accepted the shirt and track pants without a word and slipped past Jordon.

A light blue T-shirt replaced Jordon's gray windbreaker, and the muscles in his face twitched. "I'm sorry." He sounded sincere, even managed to look her in the eye.

She'd been taught to give forgiveness as easily as she gave acceptance, but this was absurd. If it weren't for that precious young man who harbored horrific sadness, she would be on the next plane home.

Until then, Maggie would keep her distance.

Wanting to get away, she walked toward the room's only exit, where she attempted to slip between Jordon and the door frame like Carlos had. But Jordon didn't step aside. Instead, he wrapped an arm around her waist and pressed her to his chest.

Maggie braced for a surge of negative energy, only to have every nerve ending in her body sing until her knees buckled and her breathing stopped.

As if life wasn't already crazy enough, now she was attracted to Jordon Kemmons.

*

Talking was Jordon's noble intention before he pulled her to his chest and set off a blast of hot lust so powerful he struggled not to act.

"You should let go of me," she whispered. Giant eyes searched his face, and little sprays of her staccato breath bounced against his hungry lips.

He knew he should be glad that one of them had the presence of mind to end the insanity. Still, he found himself releasing her amid swirls of disappointment. "Maggie, I..."

"Dr. Collins." She took two steps back and bumped against the utility sink.

"*Maggie.*" He shoved a hand through his hair. "It doesn't matter what I call you, I'm still going to struggle with things."

"Because you think I'm a promiscuous flake?" Fine lines stacked on her forehead, and the edges of her soft-leather eyes dipped.

"I never called you a flake."

"But you think it. I can tell."

"And you think I'm close-minded and evil, which doesn't sit well with me. Then again, I've given you ample reason to think those things. Correct?"

She dropped her head and pinned her eyes to his chest. "Just because a woman doesn't wear a bra doesn't mean she's promiscuous."

The corners of his mouth lifted. "Understood. And just because a man is serious and inclined to ask pointed questions to which he expects specific answers doesn't mean he's evil."

Maggie raised her head. "Of course."

He was right, but so was she, and she was also...beautiful. Dangerously beautiful. The kind of beautiful that made men do crazy things. Jordon was right there on the edge, ready to jump when she told him to, and that was why he wanted her—needed her—to be flaky or promiscuous. Either characteristic helped him rationalize his behavior. Flaky meant he could continue to convince himself that he couldn't stand to be around her. And if flaky failed to keep him in line, promiscuous meant if things went too far, there would be no negative repercussions, no guilt for his actions.

But after watching her take genuine care of Carlos and after holding her in his arms, Jordon knew without a doubt, Dr. Maggie Collins was neither flaky nor promiscuous, and he was in serious trouble.

CHAPTER SIX

Maggie couldn't sleep. She missed her bed. She missed her mother. And she had no desire to spend another night tormented by a possessed arachnid.

The anger she felt for Jordon earlier in the day chipped away at her spiritual foundation, but that was nothing compared to the jolt of electricity she felt in his arms. Visions of his dark body sprawled across the iron bed filled her weakened mind.

She tried meditation. She tried chanting. She even spent ten minutes in a head stand, hoping to dump thoughts of him from her brain.

Pulling the soft bedding over her body, she gave in and contemplated the peculiar situation. Crystal raised Maggie to be free in word and deed, which meant Maggie thought what she wanted to think and did what she wanted to do. Sometimes she wanted to have sex with men who simply stirred her desire. But never with a man like Jordon.

He was dark where every other man she'd been with had been light. And he was paying her—a lot—to do an important job, a job that provided her with enough money to finally achieve some stability in her chaotic life. Sleeping with him served no other purpose than to scratch an itch, and that simply wasn't a good enough reason to risk mental, professional, and spiritual health.

She threw the blankets off and filled with shame. Jordon's talk about promiscuity must have bothered her more than she realized. Sitting and twisting her legs over the edge of the mattress, she decided wearing something to bed in someone else's house was more respectful than wearing nothing at all. She tugged a yoga tee over her head and pulled a pair of spandex leggings over her narrow hips. As she did, she felt foolish for compromising her beliefs. She'd been sleeping naked since she was born. It was as natural to her as breathing. And since she wasn't dressed for sleep, she didn't expect to get any.

She was dressed for yoga.

The house was dark as Maggie made her way to the deck with blanket in hand. She pushed outside, taking a gust of chilly wind to the face, and her skin pimpled. In the distance, water lapped at the rock walls bordering the property.

The night stretched out before her, cool, calm, and endless. Dense cloud cover blocked the moon and stars. She smoothed the blanket in a sliver of light that started in the house and spilled onto the deck, running across the horizontal planks until it reached a privacy screen that Maggie now knew separated the main deck from the master suite. She remembered no curtains or blinds hid Jordon while he slept, and she had the overwhelming urge to behold the image.

Flake. She grimaced at the insult and sat in the middle of the blanket, forming a pretzel with her legs.

A scraping noise stopped her mid-meditation. She froze, listening to the sound of footsteps creaking over the wood. When she looked in the direction of the noises, she saw nothing but emptiness.

The rational explanation was Jordon on his side of the privacy screen, but her heart raced as though she expected something else. She stood and tiptoed across the planks until she reached the wall. "Jordon, is that you?"

"No. It's a giant spider who's waiting to attack."

For some reason, his words spoken through a raspy half-whisper left her feeling defenseless. She knew he attempted humor. She knew he wasn't a spider about to pounce, and yet she gawked around her feet, as if she expected him to scurry under the crack. "You're not funny."

Maggie agonized through his extended pause and contemplated walking away. The rolling sound of lake water mixed with her uneasiness.

"What are you doing up this late?" He spoke a little louder, but not loud enough to chase the tingles from her skin.

"What are *you* doing up this late?"

He exhaled loudly. "There you go again, answering my question with a question. I hate that."

His words were strong and his tone exasperated, but for some reason she smiled. "Sorry. I couldn't sleep."

"Neither could I."

She wished he would speak in his full voice. The vulnerability in his whisper made her stomach do silly things. Pushing the heel of her hand to her belly button, she scrambled for something to say. "Well, since neither one of us can sleep, I suppose we could not sleep together."

More silence. She expected it, grimacing the minute the collection of harmless words crossed her lips.

Jordon made a rough sound, not a laugh, something else entirely, something that made her wonder about the sounds he made in bed.

"Maggie, if I was a big bad spider that wouldn't leave you alone, what would you say to me?"

With inappropriate thoughts filling her head, she took a step closer to the wall and pressed her palms to the splintered wood. Her dry mouth hovered above a crack in the shadowy planks. "I would say, 'I like you. I do. You're a beautiful, powerful creature, but you frighten me, and I'm worried one of us will get hurt if you keep coming around." He made the noise again, and she crumbled, collapsing against the barrier between them. "Please, stay away. We'll both be a lot…happier.'"

She scanned the boards at her feet as she waited for his reply.

"Do most spiders listen?"

"They do." She was filled with a sadness she didn't understand. The dark sky wrapped around her, and instead of offering a cloak of comfort, it weighed oppressively.

"How'd you do it, Maggie?"

"Do what?"

"Get Carlos to stop crying and start eating?"

A little heaviness lifted as a cleaner image materialized—Carlos beaming over a pile of folded laundry. "We still have far to go, but the recent progress has been simple. I spent time with him. People need to feel like they're worth something. There's nothing more important to spend on a person than time."

"The biggest names in sports psychology couldn't make progress like this. What you've done is miraculous."

"I wouldn't go that far. The most profound breakthrough came when he let me help with his laundry. Otherwise, thank Goddess for TV."

She dropped to the deck and crossed her legs underneath her thighs, pressing her back against the wall. She counted five deep inhales before he spoke again.

"Well, whatever you call it, I'm impressed. It's more than I could do."

"No, you could've done it if you were here more."

"You sound like Bethany."

She crossed her arms around her chest and rubbed her hands along her cool skin. "Who's Bethany?"

"My ex-wife. She was always riding me about being gone or glued to my phone or emotionally unavailable, as she called it."

He seemed to be all of those things, and Maggie imagined most women would have a difficult time feeling secure with a man whose attentions were split. Funny, those things didn't top her list of worries about Jordon. The halo of darkness that was his constant companion bothered her more. If she could figure out why it was there...

"Jordon, I wasn't criticizing you. I was merely pointing out that my progress with Carlos isn't supernatural. It's the byproduct of being with him."

Talking like this, cloaked in darkness without the undue pressure of his eyes and separated by an impenetrable barrier, Maggie relied on intuition as her guide. In the stillness, the night air nipped at her skin, and something else tormented her. Maybe Carlos wasn't the only one hurting. "Do you like being an agent?" she prodded.

"Immensely."

"Then you owe no apologies for the steps you take to be successful."

"Maybe, but I've burned a lot of bridges over the course of my career. The general consensus is that I'm a pretty bad guy. They don't call me the 'Devil of Contract Negotiation' for nothing."

She'd thought of him as the devil a time or two... "Does the reputation bother you?"

Delving into other peoples' psyches came naturally to Maggie. She wanted to know what made them tick and how she could help. Crystal called it saving souls, but even Crystal would wilt at the seemingly insurmountable odds of saving this man.

"It doesn't bother the agent, but it bothers the man."

Maggie was starting to get glimpses of a man who cared about more than being right and making money, which was good for Carlos. The young man deserved to be more than someone's meal ticket. And Jordon—despite the ominous exterior—deserved happiness too. She closed her eyes and shook her head, moving closer to a man she should be keeping away from.

"Truth in word and deed is a difficult concept for human beings," she explained. "We have a tendency to split ourselves into pieces in order to survive. We have one side we show our friends, one side we show our colleagues, another side for our family, another side for our lovers. It's sad and exhausting, but it's sometimes a necessary evil. I think it's that way for you."

"Evil, huh?"

It was her turn to quiet.

"Maggie, do you really think I'm evil?"

At one point, she did. But now... She hung her head. If he wasn't evil, then why did she feel like crying?

"You don't have to answer that." He moved on the other side of the wall, and she imagined him walking away.

"Jordon, wait. I don't think you're evil. There's a darkness there that I can't explain, and it makes me...uncomfortable."

"Like the spider."

"I suppose." She gulped. *Save me.* Could the spider in her dreams be Jordon?

"Then I'll do my best to stay out of your way."

Maggie expected relief, but she swept away on a wave of sadness that lingered long after she fell asleep.

When she woke, she figured Jordon would be gone, flying off to another exotic location in search of his next big thing, which was good. She needed to focus on getting Carlos to the point where she could go home and still help him get well from afar.

What wasn't good was the warm glow she felt when she found Jordon, scrambling eggs on the Hibachi grill in the kitchen.

Carlos sat at the island, buttering toast. She'd never noticed before, but there were similarities between the two men. While Carlos's skin was much darker than Jordon's, they both shared the same onyx hair. Jordon's was cut clean, but longer around the edges, and Carlos wore his nearly shaved. While Jordon's body loomed thicker and infinitely stronger as a result of regular food, both men sported defined muscles and shared a height over six feet.

And today, both men wore nothing but athletic shorts.

Her gaze lingered on the puckers of muscle stacking up Jordon's abdomen. A thin strip of dark hair spilled from his navel and disappeared into the waistband of his shorts. Her heart fluttered.

"Morning, gentlemen."

Carlos turned his head and smiled. "Jordon caught a fish for breakfast."

Jordon didn't acknowledge her. She felt disappointed by both actions. "You fish?"

"I do."

His prickly demeanor fueled her foul mood. "And you kill what you catch?"

"Sometimes." He cracked an egg in one hand.

"Why not throw the poor creature back after you prove your power and buy an already murdered fish from the supermarket?"

He saw her now, his eyes bleak. "Because *evil* men do *evil* things."

Carlos pushed away from the island and left the kitchen.

"Wait, don't go." Maggie scurried after him, but not before she leveled Jordon with a look she hoped was every bit as lethal as driving a stake through his blackened heart.

By the time Maggie reached Carlos, he stood at the end of his bed, untangling headphones. She knocked on the jamb. "Can I come in?"

He didn't answer.

Maggie stepped forward. "This…thing between Jordon and me has nothing to do with you."

Carlos looked over his shoulder, blinked and returned his attention to the knotted wires.

"Jordon and I are two very different people who should steer clear of each other. Like oil and water, you know?" She tried to laugh to lighten the mood. The sound landed hollow, even in her ears. "I wanted you to know in case you thought we were fighting about you."

He looked again, slid the headphones over his ears and crawled into bed.

*

Maggie couldn't hate Jordon any more than he already hated himself. He was cold, calculating, and manipulative, and he used every one of those miserable personality traits to lure Maggie here—and then to keep her away. If it hadn't been for that damn belly dance…

He squished a pile of drippy yellow eggs underneath a metal spatula.

She stirred something in him that had disappeared since Bethany walked away with half his net worth. Maggie stirred something in him, all right—something in his pants—and the adolescent reaction disgusted him. Not too long ago, he sat at a linen-covered table, sipping Grey Goose and tonic, hoping he'd drink enough and she'd drink enough to end up naked together in his hotel room. Of course, the good doctor didn't drink. She danced, and he ended up in bed alone.

The next morning, he told himself he didn't care. She wasn't his type and he didn't need another woman leading him down the road to financial ruin. He explained away his physical reaction with the help of words like 'hussy'. And life went on. He signed new clients, checked on old clients and negotiated contracts worth more than two hundred million dollars that Bethany couldn't touch.

Things that remained elusive to most men fell at his feet: money, power, and women. He spent the money, wielded the power, but pushed the gold diggers away. All the while, he fantasized about Maggie from a safe distance.

Bringing her to North Carolina amounted to a desperate and dangerous tactic. Desperate, because Jordon hoped she was what Carlos needed. Dangerous, because she was what Jordon wanted.

He pushed the crunchy brown eggs onto a platter and cut the power to the grill. His mood was as dark and cold as the coffee in his mug. He swallowed it anyway.

Blaming Bethany for his current bitterness grew old. She didn't seem to be scarred by the divorce. In fact, she moved on quickly and completely. Last he heard, she married the louse she cheated with…and they were pregnant. He imagined how round and lush she looked carrying around the proof of her indiscretion.

Bethany had never wanted a child with him, preferring to blame his schedule for their lack of success: "You have to be home to have sex, and you have to have sex to make a baby." Be that as it may, Jordon was glad they never procreated. The world could only handle so many spoiled, evil spawn.

As if on cue, Maggie reappeared. Her dark, damp hair spiked off a forehead that wrinkled with what Jordon could only assume was disgust, and her saucer-shaped eyes appeared flat and worn.

"Are you trying to undo everything?" she asked.

Not everything. Only the buttons on her blouse. His journey started innocently enough, noting her discontent, but when he sloped down her regal nose to her pouty lips, the road took a perilous detour. Dropping his gaze off her upturned chin, he let it caress her long neck and then linger in the dip of her throat. He knew the sightseeing should end there, but the warning sounds in his head were no match for the rising heat in his lower half.

"I'm afraid Carlos thinks we're fighting because of him, and if we don't do something drastic, we're going to be right back to fishing him out of the lake."

Jordon agreed. He tossed the spatula into the sink and watched her body jolt at the sound of metal clanging against metal. She seemed to sense the danger and straightened her back. The rigid posture forced her breasts against her T-shirt, and the rest of Jordon's body reacted as swiftly and violently as the hard-on in his pants.

He charged her, closing the gap in three strides. "How's this for drastic?"

Wrapping both arms around her waist, he pinned her against his chest and covered her parted lips with his. His momentum forced him forward until her back pressed against the fridge, where he welcomed the extra support. On a volcanic wave of need, he plunged his tongue into her warm, wet mouth, giving in to temptation.

Maggie didn't fight him. Instead, she raised her smooth leg alongside the clenched muscles of his thigh and laced her tongue with his. She danced her hands over his bare back, setting off sparks beneath his skin, and then she clawed him with her nails.

The sting elicited a throaty roar.

Hearing his own desire, Jordon's need turned primal. Her pulsing, swirling tongue teased him with the promise of hot, earthy sex. He swallowed against her open mouth, tasting all she had to offer—warmth like the sun, a rush like the wind and wetness like the rain.

She arched her back and rocked against his groin, wrapping her leg tighter around his hip, making him want more than he possibly deserved.

It'd been so long…too long.

Dragging his lips across her jaw, Jordon sunk his teeth into her lobe. She moaned, and the sound of pleasure urged him on, deeper and harder. He pressed a palm to the pointed tip of her breast, brushing back and forth. And when she moaned again, he felt woozy, his head spinning as he dragged his mouth back to capture hers.

Jordon worked through the stifling heat to slip his hand beneath her shirt, moving over the smooth skin of her stomach, inching closer and closer until his fingertips brushed the bare curve of breast. While his heart pounded in his chest, he teased her nipple, flicking with his thumb.

She opened her mouth wider and knotted long arms around his neck. As her hands massaged his scalp, her leg clamped around his lower half, and all he could think about was sex. Against his fridge.

His thoughts hovered over them like a depraved observer with visions of driving deep while her long limbs draped and gripped his body. It would've been hot, had it not been so desperate.

*

When Jordon backed away, Maggie stayed pressed against the refrigerator, mostly for balance. She didn't trust herself to walk on solid ground after that earthquake. Lowering a foot to the floor, she pressed fingers to her bruised lips.

"That was very drastic," she said, startled by the shake in her voice. She watched his chest convulse, and worried he might hyperventilate too. "Are you okay?"

"No."

Confusion set in. Although, she hadn't initiated the contact, he obviously thought she'd done something wrong. "I'm sorry. I should've behaved better."

His eyes narrowed to slits. "You behaved pretty damn well."

"But you're upset. I can tell. Your eyes are…dark."

"Are you scared?"

"Yes." She felt like crying. A ball of emotion sat on her chest and made it hard to breathe. And yet, she didn't feel at risk of hyperventilating.

What was happening to her?

"You should be scared." He crossed his strong arms over the tight curls scattered across his chest, but it didn't help Maggie feel better. He was still shirtless and very aroused.

Her confusion turned to panic before this unreadable man. No intuition, no empathy, no psychic premonitions or energy shields seemed powerful enough to protect her. Every false sense of security she relied upon for the last twenty-eight years failed.

"You're in over your head, Maggie. Carlos needs help, but you do, too." He poked a finger at her through the charged air.

He could've hit her and she wouldn't have felt a thing. "Why do I need help? I don't understand."

Grunting, he closed his eyes and shook his head. "Never mind."

She was getting used to living with the unrest. Dark emotions quickened and strengthened until they overshadowed her trademark optimism. "No. Tell me why. Why should I be scared? Why do I need help?" Her body trembled, and her nails bit into her palm.

He opened his eyes and stared at her, a blank stare made worse by his rigid posture. How could he dam his emotions while her heart thrashed and a simple breath was torture?

Pushing a palm over her convulsing heart, Maggie chose to end the torment. "Forget it. I don't care. I'm done here."

Bare feet slapped the hardwoods as she raced to the front door, wanting to run far away from Jordon. But when a door slammed above her, she remembered why she was here. Carlos.

How much of the argument had he heard?

Frozen at the front door with a trembling hand on the knob, she realized she wasn't even sure where to go. Barefoot and crying, someone was bound to pick her up and admit her to the nearest mental hospital.

Maggie leaned against the door and filled her lungs with air. After what happened in the kitchen, she couldn't imagine Jordon balking at her request for him to hire another therapist, so she'd start there. Once she knew Carlos was taken care of, she could leave this chaos behind.

Making her way back into the kitchen for Round Two, Maggie dreaded facing Jordon. But he was gone when she got there. One glance at the refrigerator, and she remembered the way he touched, the way he tasted. Her body burned at the memory of those delirious moments before his mood soured.

They were nothing like oil and water.

She scanned the lake landscape beyond the dining room and

settled her gaze on the end of the pier. Jordon stood straight and tall like Poseidon. She feared another confrontation, but the open, aching part of her wanted words to make things right.

When Maggie reached the wooden planks that hovered inches off the murky lake, her goose pimples returned. Such dramatic events surrounded this body of water, this house and that man.

Jordon shoved hands into his short pockets and pinned his eyes on the horizon. "You're under no obligation to stay. I won't hold you to the contract."

Maggie gulped. "Okay."

"And I'm sorry," he said with a shake of his head.

When he looked at her and held her gaze, she felt his silent plea. "What's going on, Jordon? Tell me."

The muscles of his back flexed as he bent and sat on the edge of the pier, dropping his feet into the water. He sat there for the longest time, his shoulders slumping further with every breath. "I haven't been with a woman since Bethany left me, mostly because I've convinced myself all women are a threat to my success and sanity."

No matter the reason, it was hard to believe a handsome, single, successful man who rocked a body like his wasn't enjoying an active post-divorce sex life. The idea that Maggie's middle-aged mother had more sex than Jordon disgusted her. And yet, his struggle with intimacy wasn't unusual. "Lots of people go through dry spells after a divorce."

"Yeah, well, in case you didn't notice, my dry spell is pushing me over the edge." He dropped his head to his hands. "I'm so sorry, Maggie."

She walked toward him and settled by his side, her elbow bumping his bare skin as her feet dipped into the cool water. "It's okay."

"No, it's not. I treated you like a slab of meat."

Maybe, but the mere memory of his intensity turned her on,

and the heat between her legs warned her against reminiscing with Jordon by her side. Her impulsive streak couldn't be trusted.

"In case you didn't notice, I didn't mind," she said, smiling, hoping the admission delivered with humor would brighten his outlook and diffuse some of her heat.

His cheeks caved and his dark brows pinched together over his nose. "Would you mind if I did it again?"

She felt winded. "I, uh…"

He looked at her, and the muscles in his face softened. "I know you want to leave. Hell, you probably should leave, but God help me, I can't stop myself from wanting you to stay."

Maggie raised a hand to her mouth to hide her shock.

"And it has nothing to do with Carlos." Jordon stared at her lips. "Tell me you feel it, too, Maggie. There is something very powerful between us."

She laid a hand on his fabulous thigh and fought back a whimper. "I do. I find you terribly attractive." She winced at the honesty and the vulnerability in her voice. "We obviously have… chemistry, but I'm here to help Carlos."

"Right." Jordon looked back over the lake and leaned forward, tossing a handful of water into the air. "Why can't you be here for both?"

She gulped and stared at an expanding circle of water left over from the splash. "I don't know. It seems…seedy."

"There's nothing seedy about two consenting adults enjoying each other's company." He smiled, a beautiful soul-melting smile. "I want you, Maggie, and when I want something, I get it. Morally ambiguous or not. That's just the kind of guy I am."

With his smile burning a hole in her heart, she nodded. If this much passion and magnetism existed between them when they were holding back, she could only imagine the combustion when they stopped fighting.

She matched the flirtatious curve of his lips. "My mother raised me to be open minded to situations other people find morally ambiguous."

"Like plural marriage?" he teased.

"Exactly." Her smile broadened, but then she groaned. Her mother's entanglement with Paul wasn't really funny.

Jordon kicked up a gentle swell of water and looked her over, slowly, closely, like he was reading the pages of a sacred book. "But you aren't interested in a life of moral ambiguity, are you?" His warm hand slipped up her arm, skirted her shoulder and rested on her neck.

"No."

"What are you interested in, Maggie?"

She struggled to think straight against the startling sensation of his thumb sliding back and forth over her bottom lip. "Saving my soul."

He smiled again. "Will you save mine first?"

CHAPTER SEVEN

Jordon would've plunged more than his tongue inside of Maggie if Bernie hadn't interrupted the start of a perfect kiss.

"Carlos called me to take him to a hotel. He says he's causing problems between you two." Bernie snorted. "Although, at the moment, I'm not seeing any problems."

Maggie looked at Jordon with those sultry cartoon eyes, and he cursed their loss of privacy.

"We can't let him leave." She stood up with such a jolt, the pier rocked.

Jordon steadied her swaying body with an arm around her waist. "What do you want to do about it?"

"We need to present a united front. He needs to know that we care about him." She took off toward the house with her shoulders back and her hips rocking.

Bernie chuckled. "Boss Man, you've got your hands full with that one."

Jordon liked the image. His hands full of Maggie. Maggie full of him. He shook off the lusty thoughts and slapped Bernie's shoulder. "Not yet, man, but I sure as hell won't stop until I do."

Five minutes later, Jordon straddled the arm of the couch where Carlos sat with his eyes glued to the water. Behind Jordon, Bernie perched on a stool at the kitchen island.

"Carlos, Jordon and I won't be fighting anymore." Maggie paced the length of a blue Dhurrie rug. "Right, Jordon?"

Jordon's lips twitched. Her hands were on her hips and she looked down at him from her upright position. "Right, Maggie."

"Jordon and I tried to yell over our feelings instead of talking about them, but we're past that now, and we promise to work together to help you. Communication is the key to building relationships, and now that Jordon and I are talking about our feelings, there's no reason to yell. So you see, there's no reason for you to leave."

Jordon stifled a laugh. The whole thing was preposterous. Maggie preaching about relationships to a professional baseball player who could get more ass than the toilet seat at a Mexican restaurant. Meanwhile, the world's highest paid sports agent couldn't stop thinking about getting her undressed so he could get laid for the first time in two years.

He looked around the room and marveled. It was a scene out of some whacky sitcom, where one big dysfunctional family worked through their issues. Jordon scowled at the random word. This wasn't his family. He didn't have time for family. But the more Maggie talked and the more Carlos listened, the more Jordon couldn't shake the feeling that this sort of teamwork was missing from his personal life.

"You know what I think?" Maggie stopped moving and widened her eyes. "I think we need to get out of this house and have some fun." She turned to Bernie. "Do you think you and your wife can get a sitter? Jordon's taking us out tonight."

Jordon groaned. All he wanted was a quiet night at home…in bed…and not alone. But the rest of them looked so happy. What choice did he have?

If Maggie wanted a night out, she'd get her night out. And in or out, Jordon intended to get what he wanted, too.

Several hours later, Maggie filled her lungs with the warm, deep-fried-scented air swirling around the restaurant patio and admired Jordon. His shirt fell open at his throat, revealing a few black curls, but his attractive dress mismatched his surly expression.

"Despite that nasty frown, you look very handsome," she teased.

He leaned forward, carrying with him the warm spice of his aftershave. Maggie breathed him in, mesmerized by the sparks of yellow in his eyes.

"Thank you. And you look amazing, which isn't helping my mood. I wanted to stay home and come…" he dragged a breath into his open mouth, "…to an agreement."

His suggestive words and soft tone tickled her skin, forcing her back in her chair on an exhale. "An agreement about what?"

He flattened his palms on the table, his right hand inches from hers. With a stretch of his fingers, he traced her thumb. "You know what I want."

Oh, she knew. She'd have to be void of all senses to mistake his desire. Every part of his body screamed his intentions. And in case she didn't have a clue, he made it clear with a palm to her knee.

Maggie jumped at the touch of his hand, and slipped her tongue around her dry mouth, trying to focus on something other than the heat he generated. "I haven't exactly agreed to your proposition."

He moved his hand up her thigh.

She wiggled and pulled back a bit, but he tightened his grip, holding her in place, sending jolts of pleasure to her most sensitive parts.

"I can make you happy to agree." He inched his fingers along her inner thigh. "My powers of persuasion are legendary."

A roar of celebration exploded from the bocce court.

Maggie squeezed her legs shut.

Jordon sat back, his scowl darker than the moonless sky.

Biting her lip to keep from laughing at his frustration, Maggie enjoyed herself for the first time in weeks. She was finally free from the constant tension that resulted from fighting her apparent attraction to a man she deemed entirely wrong for her, body and soul. Letting go of the resistance felt closer to Good than Evil, and there were all sorts of things a free thinking and acting woman like Maggie could do to enlighten and enliven a man like Jordon.

Since the start of their second kiss on the pier, she'd thought of nothing but kissing him again. And then the talk in the living room ended with a happier Carlos, leaving Maggie to determine that everything worked better when she and Jordon worked together. She couldn't help but wonder if the theory would hold true in bed.

His gaze pierced through hers without a blink, and the muscles in his neck bunched above his starched collar. He was wound so tight. Playing too hot and too fast with a powerful man was asking for trouble. So why did she feel like begging for every ounce of trouble he had?

"Boss Man, your throw." Bernie raised a yellow ball to Jordon.

"I pass." Jordon took a swig from a brown bottle. "Carlos, watch the arm. You're behind on conditioning, and bocce'll make you throw like a girl."

Something flickered in Carlos's eyes. Fortunately, it wasn't a fresh wave of sadness. It was more like disgust, but Maggie couldn't be sure.

Instead of dwelling, she filed the observation away for later contemplation and stood, wiggling her fingers in the air. "Give it to me."

Bocce seemed like a wholesome alternative to her previous activity. She and Jordon needed some physical distance before they set the place on fire.

Bernie dropped the heavy plastic into her hand, and she made her way to the end of the court. The restaurant patio outside a North Charlotte shopping mall was Jordon's idea, something to get Carlos out of the house and back in the competitive swing.

"Hit the blue balls, Maggie. Bernie cheats." Tabitha folded her arms underneath huge breasts and flashed a gorgeous smile at the large man towering over her.

"But never on you, baby."

They kissed, and Maggie felt warm admiration followed by a twinge of sadness. She hadn't been around many married couples. Crystal avoided the "institutionally minded masses." Being with Bernie and Tabitha, watching their easy affection, Maggie couldn't help but question what she'd been raised to believe: *Romantic love is a myth created to contain and undermine greatness.*

Whose greatness, Maggie wasn't sure. Just like all the other less-than-mainstream lessons swimming around in her head, Crystal's hatred for romantic love didn't make complete sense.

"Dr. Maggie, throw."

She blinked and saw Carlos puzzling at her from across the sandy court.

"I'm...lining up," she said, clearing her head with a shake and raising her arm a couple times for proof. "Watch and learn."

Maggie swung her arm back and forward, releasing the ball into the air. She bounced on her toes as she watched the ball drop several feet short of the target.

Carlos cackled.

She'd never heard him laugh, and the joyful sound prompted laughter in return. "Hush," she said, pointing a finger across the court. "It was one bad throw. Watch your back next time."

"Tabby'll show you how it's done, Maggie." Bernie swept a hand before his wife, paving the way for her toss.

Once again, Maggie felt a mix of admiration and sadness. She glanced at Carlos, who was smiling but standing alone at the end of the court. Alone, like her. They stood in stark contrast to Bernie and Tabitha. Bernie wrapped his arm around his wiggling wife's waist, and Tabitha pressed lips to her husband's neck. They might be delusional victims of a non-existent romantic love, but they didn't seem to mind. Delusional or not, they were a pair. Partners. Soul mates.

For some stupid reason, Maggie's gaze roamed to Jordon. He sat pressed against the chair with a hand covering his mouth, eyes on her. She smiled, mostly to hide her ridiculous train of thought. But when he dragged his hand over his lips and smiled back, all thought disappeared.

Jordon stood and crossed the patio with determined strides. With each step, his smile faded until he looked very serious... very sexy. She smelled his cologne and felt the heat from his body before he grabbed her hand and tugged.

"Come with me."

Her feet tangled, and she stumbled. "Where?"

"Stop with the questions." He slipped an arm around her waist, rocketing heat throughout her body as he pulled her into the crowded restaurant and then out into the parking lot.

He moved briskly over the asphalt, and her heels wobbled as she tried to keep up. "Where are we going?"

"Somewhere."

The way he said it—all breathy and non-negotiable—stirred her imagination. *Somewhere*. She could only dream of what would happen there. "Where exactly?"

He spun around, and she bumped him chest-to-chest in the dark space between an SUV and a mini-van. He leaned close enough to tickle her lips with his ragged breath, sending hot air into her lungs, skittering over her insides until the heat pooled between her legs.

"You know what I want, Maggie, and I don't care where I get it."

She gasped. "We should talk about this."

He cocked a brow, smirked and traced a finger along her collar bone. "There are other things we should be doing with our mouths."

She couldn't move, couldn't breathe, couldn't recall ever being pursued so completely. Jordon stalked her with hungry eyes, a feathery touch and scorching words. Her body responded to the intensity, heating and melting in all the right places, making him hard to resist.

Maggie scrambled to form an intelligent sentence. "There are questions and answers we..."

"You want questions? Fine. I'll give you questions." He dipped his finger from her neck to trace the outline of her breast. "I know you don't wear a bra. Are you covered down there?" He dropped his eyes to the short hem of her dress and his fingers followed.

Maggie wobbled on her heels and had a random wish for a glass of ice. Touching the air with her tongue, she tasted Jordon on the breeze. Desire raged out of control.

With a tip of her chin to the starry sky, she gave in. "Why don't you find out?" she asked, stepping her feet apart.

He didn't wait for a second invitation.

When his hand smoothed over the inside of her thigh and his fingers brushed the soft skin between her legs, Maggie shuddered, her insides turning hot with sticky need.

Before she could worry about where they were and what they were doing, he dropped his hand from beneath her skirt and gripped her by the elbow, pulling her through the parking lot until the town car appeared.

Jordon punched a code into the driver's door and opened the locks. "Get in."

All but the front windows were dark enough to hide them. Still, Maggie hesitated. She recognized the line she was about to cross and thought—for a split second—about changing directions, but he pressed a hand to her bottom and smoothed his palm over her curves.

"Get in the car, Maggie."

Fanning the tingles spreading through her body with a deep breath, she slid across the cool backseat and surrendered the minute his gorgeous face and wide shoulders came into view. He crawled toward her, stalking her from beneath hooded eyes.

Impulse shattered anticipation, and Maggie grabbed his face between her hands. Pulling him to her, she crushed his mouth with her lips.

Passion turned into a struggle when Jordon leaned his full weight against her and Maggie's head and neck bent against the door. She tossed her right ankle over the front seat, trying to get comfortable, concentrating on the way his kisses stole her breath and stirred her desire. But as the seconds ticked by, her body screamed for release from the cramped space and clothing.

She imagined shedding her dress, stripping him slowly and feeling him skin to skin.

With her fingers spread over his chest, she grazed the hard points of his nipples against her palms. He moaned at the simple pressure, reminding Maggie that she wasn't the only one who wanted release. She was making out in an uncomfortable car with a man who was sex starved.

She'd have to speed things up.

Moving her hands to the button of his pants, she worked until she held him. "I want you inside me."

He groaned, breathing hot and wet against her neck, but he didn't make a move to lift her skirt and end his misery. Instead, he wasted precious time, licking a trail along her jaw to her ear, where he nibbled, causing tiny pinpricks of pleasure to cover her body, threatening her ability to give.

"Now," she rasped, tightening her hand around his erection.

Jordon froze, breathing loudly in her ear. A second later, he pushed up and sat back against the opposite door, glowering but looking incredibly sexy while he did.

Maggie drew a few quick breaths and swallowed her confusion. "What's wrong?"

His face contorted and his eyes rolled skyward. He growled, and she wondered if he was experiencing a bout of performance anxiety. If he was, she had the anecdote.

Pulling her leg off the front seat and settling into a kneeling position on the carpeted floor, Maggie patted the leather. "Sit."

He hesitated.

She stretched toward him and tugged on the waistband of his pants, sliding the fabric over his hot skin to maneuver around the proof of his lingering desire. "I said sit."

This time, he did as he was told, and the mini-power trip thrilled her. She imagined few people got Jordon Kemmons to obey…but she did.

Maggie flashed a sly smile and gripped his swollen penis, letting the power and electricity heat her blood. She heard his head hit the back of the seat with a moan as soon as her lips brushed across his sensitive tip. Rolling her tongue over the top and around the edge, she concentrated on giving him pleasure.

When she took him completely into her mouth, he slid a hand through her hair and massaged her neck. "Maggie."

Edging closer to orgasm when he whispered her name, she pressed her thighs together to feed the luscious spasms.

With the next sweep of her tongue, he gripped the hair at the base of her neck, tugging gently on the roots. Maggie whimpered as she worked him over, pumping her mouth until a large portion of Jordon's pent-up sexual frustration released.

She lingered between his legs, feeling the thick muscles in his thighs relax beneath her hands. She would've stayed there longer, savoring her power, had someone not knocked on the window.

Several silent seconds passed as Jordon reassembled his pants. Maggie waited for him to say something, anything. Thank you, maybe… nope. He grunted a couple times as he dressed, but otherwise said nothing to acknowledge Maggie's presence or gift.

This was not how she expected their encounter to go—or end. As usual, she felt confused and frustrated by his actions and reactions. When he rolled down the window, she struggled to look innocent when she felt anything but.

"Boss Man, we can't find Carlos."

How did anyone doubt karma?

Jordon leaped from the town car, leaving Maggie behind. He

flashed his eyes between every car, under every truck. "What happened?"

Bernie weaved in and out of the parked cars behind him. "He got a phone call, and he left to take it. Tabby and I went to look for him when he didn't come back."

"Why am I the warden?" Jordon bit into the F-word with an anger uncharacteristic even for him. Maggie's fault. She was too deep in his head. He should be one-hundred-percent focused on Carlos. Instead, he was nursing wounds from what did or didn't happen in the back seat of his car.

Why did he care? He got what he wanted, didn't he? Sure, the pleasure was one-sided, but he knew better than most people that life wasn't balanced. He also wasn't a soft-hearted guy. Walking away from the negotiation table with his needs met was what mattered most, wasn't it? Then why was he hung up on Maggie's willingness to bypass the foreplay and get right to the main event?

He charged the pavement in the opposite direction of Bernie and Maggie, needing space. His breath came heavy like a bull's. While he walked alone, scanning the parking lot for Carlos, he tried his damnedest to push thoughts of the aggravating woman he was trying to outrun from his head. He failed. Miserably.

He didn't get it. She'd been all over him in the kitchen. He expected the same enthusiasm in the car. *Damn!* If he'd suspected for one minute that being honest with her would demote him to a pitiful psych patient, he would've kept his mouth shut and continued to brood from a distance.

Clenching his teeth together, Jordon swore under his breath. He wished he could muster some high-and-mighty principles when it came to Maggie. The simple fact that he invited her to North Carolina after months of fantasizing about her proved how weak he was, and then he confirmed it in the backseat of the town car by letting her take control. He wanted the release enough to sell the soul she didn't think he had.

Up ahead, the parking lot ended at a row of trees. Beyond the shadows, street lamps and headlights flickered. If Carlos was out there, Jordon wasn't going to find him by chance. He reached into his front pocket for his phone, hoping the kid would answer.

Before Jordon could dial, the screen lit up with Bernie's text. *Found him.*

Jordon veered right, making his way back toward the lights of the shopping mall, while Bernie described their exact location in a follow-up text. A few minutes later, Jordon saw Maggie with her bony knees and long legs scrunched on the curb, and Carlos lying belly-up on the grass. Jordon snarled and quickened the pace, passing Bernie and feeling angrier with every step.

Maggie must've seen him coming and sensed his mood, because she stood and walked toward him with a frustrating calm. "It's all good. Why don't you and Bernie bring the car around?"

That damn short dress...and those damn high heels. He'd never met a woman who flaunted her uniqueness in such an overtly sexual manner. He knew it wasn't rational, but he wanted to punish her for his loss of control, for making him feel more than he expected. The images in his mind turned lusty and bordered on perverse. When Jordon noticed Tabitha lurking in the shadows, he was reminded that turning Maggie's bare ass over his knee wasn't his top concern.

He sidestepped her. "Carlos, get up."

"Jordon, don't. Not here." Maggie grabbed his wrist, but he pulled free.

"Get up now. This pisses me off. What the hell is going on?" He bent over the young man, who still looked like a boy with watery eyes and quivering bottom lip. Emotion tugged on Jordon's heart. "I'm sorry. Don't cry. Please, don't cry. Come on, man. Guys don't cry."

Jordon didn't care what the suit cost or that the ground was damp from the underground sprinkler system. He dropped to his knees and sat down next to Carlos. "We can fix this—whatever it is."

Carlos blinked.

The kid obviously didn't want to talk, and Jordon was happy to oblige. "How about we forget it ever happened? I won't say another word if you get up, get in the car and stop crying."

On a shaky exhale, Carlos rolled to his side and sat.

"Thatta boy." Jordon smacked his back and looked smugly at Maggie who was shaking her head, giant silver hoops dangling from the lobes he'd been nibbling.

With a shove, Jordon pushed off the wet grass to stand. He watched Carlos and Tabitha slide into the car. And then he saw Maggie, sauntering toward him. He had half a mind to walk away.

"Just once I'd like to hear you support the kid without demeaning him," she said.

Jordon scoffed. "Who cares how I did it? I got him into the car, didn't I? The end result is what matters." If that was what he believed, then why was he so bothered by his inability to keep her entertained in the backseat of his car? He got the end result of most men's dreams.

Maggie took a half-step back and blinked a few times. "I disagree. I think the journey matters as much as the destination. I also disagree with your take on male emotion. I've seen plenty of enlightened men cry."

Jordon wanted to call her a liar, because if she cared at all about *the journey* she wouldn't have rushed what they shared. And please, enlightened men crying? There wasn't even a response for that.

He walked before he said something he'd regret, but she stopped his forward motion with a hand to his back. "Did I do something wrong?"

Once again, he thought about telling her, but then he realized they were on display for the occupants of the town car. Besides, he wasn't the kind of guy who admitted his weaknesses. Each time he did, someone used them against him.

Jordon shook his head. "No, Maggie. It was me. I misunderstood what was happening between us." He bit his bottom lip, having said more than he wanted to say.

"What *is* happening between us?"

Her question hung heavy between them, but the ache in Jordon's chest wasn't enough to produce an answer. "No more questions," he said. "You'll have to figure things out on your own."

He walked away, even more frustrated than he'd been earlier in the evening. When he reached the car and slumped inside, he slammed the car door, wishing he could do the same to his rusty heart.

CHAPTER EIGHT

The spider sat on Maggie's thigh. She tried to scream, but her lips fused shut. She tried to move, but her limbs went limp.

Save me.

Thoughts formed. She looked around her office for Crystal or Paul...even Carlos, while her heart thudded an unsettling beat. She blinked and jumped to the purple velvet sofa, while the spider scurried across the floor.

Save me.

Maggie looked for a cup to catch him in. He slipped beneath the door as her heart roared in her ears. She followed him into the hall...but she wasn't in the hall. The spider raced across Jordon's loft, bolting underneath the poker table. She willed her feet to follow despite distant warnings, and ended outside a closed door, hand on the knob. When she opened the door, the spider sat in the middle of Jordon's bed.

Save me.

Maggie forced her eyes open and snapped out of the dream. She sat, threw aside the covers and bit back a scream. After what she'd been through tonight, she needed peaceful sleep. Instead, her mind continued to torment her with visions of spiders that led to Jordon, when Jordon wanted nothing more to do with her.

Humpf! Maggie glared at the clock. Two hours passed since she extracted herself from the mausoleum of a living room where Carlos and Jordon watched sports television until they drooled. Nobody spoke. If it weren't for her genuine interest in whether or not Carlos had recovered from his unexpected relapse, she would've locked herself inside her room upon arrival.

She stilled and listened. When she first climbed into bed, she could hear the television rumbling below her. Now, nothing but silence slipped through the floor boards. Good. Everyone in their own bed. Where they belonged. Not that there was another option. Not that she expected to sleep anywhere else. What happened in the car was...

What was it, Maggie? She reached behind her, pinched a pillow and pitched it across the room. *It was stupid.*

She knew she could come up with better descriptors than one that made her sound like a five-year-old, but the alternate descriptions weren't exactly supporting her initial claim. While her head thought her actions in the car were stupid, her body and her heart felt...other things.

What happened in the car was more power and passion than she'd enjoyed in a long time. Shaking her head as she stood to stretch, Maggie hoped Jordon was having similar thoughts. Weeding through them could be the thing keeping him agitated. She frowned at her attempt to rationalize his rude behavior, but then reminded herself she wasn't making excuses for him—she was analyzing what was happening between them.

What *was* happening between them?

She shook her head again, hoping to scatter some of the confusion, but the questions settled in the same order. Was she helping Jordon get back on the proverbial horse? Maggie choked a little on the dirty thought. Or was she scratching her own festering itch? Maybe a little of both. Did it matter?

Forcing a blast of air over loose lips, she wanted to focus on Carlos and leave Jordon alone. But since the latter proved impossible, there was obviously something brewing between them beyond Jordon's need for sex and her desire to help him heal. Wasn't there? Maggie pinched the bridge of her nose and wished she could stop thinking of new questions when she hadn't thought of answers for the old ones. Jordon wanted her to figure the answers out on her own, but she wasn't having much luck. She would rather figure them out with him.

Smoothing the hem of her poet's blouse over her backside, Maggie crossed to the door. The V-neck slipped off one shoulder and she patted the cotton into place, tiptoeing past Carlos's room. By the time she'd descended the stairs, the fabric slipped again, and she lifted a hand to the ruffle but froze when she saw Jordon. The room was dark, the television quiet. He was wide awake, an empty tumbler in hand.

"Hi." She stepped toward him.

He didn't speak, simply leaned forward and set his glass on the table.

Maggie refused to be deterred. She moved to the sofa and curled a leg underneath her before sitting beside him. The sound of his breathing mixed with the questions in her head.

She drew a breath, and her exhale echoed in the silence. "I…" She breathed in and out again. "Jordon, I think…" *Ugh!* Why couldn't she say something meaningful? She rolled her eyes to the ceiling before trying again. "I'm struggling here."

Better. The words weren't perfect, but they were honest and formed a complete sentence.

He turned to face the black beyond the glass. "Let me help you out, Maggie. You're struggling because I don't *do it* for you. Being with me in the car set you straight on a few things, like maybe there's a reason Jordon hasn't had sex for a while, it's because he's…"

She grabbed his arm. "Stop it. You're being ridiculous."

He turned narrowed eyes on her. "Am I? You sure as hell couldn't get it over with fast enough."

The words stunned her. Was that what she projected? "Jordon, it was the backseat of a car. I'm not exactly short. I had a cramp in my neck and a charlie horse in my thigh, and you had…to hurry."

His laughter rumbled the emptiness between them. "Seriously? If the only things you felt were cramps and the need to hurry, then I must be worse than I thought." He looked away again.

Maggie rubbed her hand up his arm and scooted closer. "You're not. That's not what I meant. Jordon, look at me." She reached for his jaw and turned his head. When his eyes connected with hers, she felt a jolt. Heat spread over her cheeks, cascading down her chest to swirl in her belly. Her lips twitched and she almost kissed him as proof, but where would that lead? Probably someplace neither one of them was ready to go...yet. She sighed. "I feel much more than cramps when I'm with you."

He smiled slowly, deliberately, his gaze coming to rest on her lips. "Is this some sort of psychobabble meant to calm my narcissistic rage?"

"I don't think you're narcissistic."

His smile broadened and he pressed his hands to either side of her neck. "Then what do you think of me?"

At the moment, lots of thoughts came to mind, but Maggie could barely swallow let alone speak. "Jordon?"

"Yes?" He dropped his voice to match hers.

"If we keep acting like this, what comes next?"

He leaned forward to brush his nose to hers. "You mean *who...* who comes next?"

His hot breath warmed her mouth, and Maggie inched her lips closer. "After the sex, Jordon. What happens then?"

"More sex." He kissed her, lips to lips—no tongue—and then lifted his mouth. "More sex." He kissed her again, slipping his hands around her shoulders, drawing her to his chest. "More sex. I think you get the idea."

She wrapped her arms around his neck, and her heart beat against his. "You're oversimplifying things."

He squeezed her tighter, and for some strange reason, the added pressure made her laugh.

"Honey, if you think being with me is simple, then you're in for a treat." He brushed his lips below her ear.

Somewhere, something vibrated. Neither one of them moved

for the longest time, but then Jordon snarled. "My phone." He pressed his lips to her forehead before he answered the call and disappeared into the darkness.

After five minutes passed, Maggie could no longer feel the warmth where his lips had been. After thirty minutes, the couch cushion regained its shape. After an hour, Maggie thought it entirely possible she imaged the whole encounter. She closed her lids, breathed deeply, and opened her eyes again. No bed. No dream. Just an empty living room and a heart filled with disappointment.

Why did she even worry about giving in to her desire for Jordon? Between her conscience, Jordon's moods, Carlos's drama and the ever-present BlackBerry, they didn't stand a chance.

*

Jordon switched the phone to his other ear and rolled his eyes. He knew the call would sour once Mason's dad got on the line. Jordon listened to a few slurred words, and contempt stewed in his gut. The guy reminded Jordon of his father.

Hearing Mason's nervous chatter in the background pulled Jordon out of his sordid memories. "Mr. Cutler, we'll wait for the MRI. Once we have results, then we know what we're dealing with."

The drunk stuttered, and Jordon cut him off. "I said we wait. In the meantime, I suggest you lay off the bottle and let Mason sleep."

Like hundreds of phone calls before, this one ended with a sloppy apology from Old Man Cutler and a woeful goodnight from Mason. Jordon tossed the phone to the right side of the bed and smacked his head on the wrought iron a few times. When the sting of the blows subsided, he thought of Maggie.

How often had his married nights ended like this?

Jordon felt powerless over the replay of history, and Maggie had no idea what she was getting into. His jaw twitched, and he pressed his thumb to his cheek to calm the throbbing Bethany hadn't known what she was in for, either. And like Bethany, he suspected Maggie wouldn't appreciate constant brush-offs. But what was he supposed to do? Ignore a long-term client for a roll in the sheets? Of course not, and any woman who expected him to choose wasn't the right woman.

He smacked his head harder this time. What the hell was he thinking? *The right woman?* When had he stopped looking at Maggie as a means to end his sexual frustration and started looking at her as a…what? Girlfriend? He released a humorless laugh. He was too damn old for a girlfriend. A…wife? He tried that before.

Maggie had great legs, the sexiest mouth he'd ever seen— or tasted—and a body made for bending. Why did he want to complicate things by pushing for something more?

Jordon rubbed a hand over his tired eyes and thought about waltzing upstairs to do the deed without saying a word just to prove his point. He figured he could get her to comply without too much resistance. Hell, in their few physical entanglements he'd learned a thing or two about crushing her resolve.

His eyelids closed. Nibbling her ear. Yeah, that heated her up. His hands rested on his rising chest, and before he could think of another spot on Maggie's delicious body, he drifted to sleep.

The next thing Jordon knew, his BlackBerry alarm buzzed from the bedside table. He showered, shaved and dragged his heavy body into a single-breasted suit, all the while wondering what the hell was different.

He took late night calls. Part of the job. He travelled. Part of the job. He carried around more stress than a suspension bridge. Also part of the job. And yet, today, before the sun even shone, he felt like shit. He thought the unrest from last night would disappear with some sleep. Obviously, he was wrong.

The unrest led him to the bottom of a staircase he didn't intend to climb. Before he thought better, he'd reached the top and stood at Maggie's door. Jordon pushed the door open to watch her sleep. She curled into an extra pillow, the sheets tangled around her feet. Miles of silky skin extended from her ankles to the riding hem of her shirt, and all he wanted to do was run his hands over every inch.

This is a bad idea.

For once, Jordon listened to the voice in his head and turned to leave.

"Is everything okay?"

Her sleepy voice stopped him cold and forced his reply. "I'm sorry to bother you."

"It's fine." She sat, pulled the sheet to her knees and her knees to her chest, and smiled a lazy smile that begged him to stay, to crawl into bed where her arms and legs could wrap around him like a cocoon. "Did you need something?"

Talk about a loaded question. Jordon roughed a palm over his wrinkled forehead, trying to remember how he got to the foot of her bed in the first place. "Again, I'm sorry. My behavior isn't making any sense lately. I should go. Bernie's waiting."

"Where are you going?"

"New York." Instead of nodding goodbye and leaving, he sat on the end of the bed as if the spot was his ultimate destination. "I have meetings scheduled."

"How long will you be gone?"

"I don't know. It all depends on the negotiations."

She dropped her chin to her knees and even in the dim light of the moon he could see her smile fade. "Okay."

He touched her—just a covered foot at first, but then his hand slid underneath the sheet to her ankle where he wrapped his fingers around the warm skin. "I'm sorry about last night."

"What are you sorry for?"

The backseat. His anger in the parking lot. His distance at home. The phone call. *All of it.* Which wasn't true. Some parts he definitely didn't regret. Some parts he wanted nothing more than to repeat and expand upon... "I'm sorry for the way I acted in the car and in the parking lot, and I'm even more sorry I had to take that call when we were just getting to a point where I could've have made it up to you."

She rubbed a palm against his shoulder, letting the tips of her fingernails nuzzle his neck. "I was disappointed, but I get it. I know what you do. I know who you are. You can no more turn that off than I can turn off what I do and who I am. You shouldn't be sorry for something you *had* to do."

A pleasant chill rolled over him. "But there was something I *wanted* to do more." He massaged her calf muscle.

"What time's your flight?" She smiled.

Her expression sparked in his chest, and he glanced at his watch, started calculating what time remained. But then he sighed. What the hell was happening to him? Bernie was in the driveway. Millions of dollars were up for grabs in New York, and he would rather stay home...in bed?

He jumped to his feet. "I'm late already." He regretted the abrupt movement the minute her smile fell, her right cheek dropping to her knee. He reached out and laid a palm on the exposed side of her face. "Will you be here when I get back?" She had a home and a life that didn't include him, and as soon as she deemed Carlos well enough for virtual therapy, she'd leave. There'd be nothing keeping her here.

Maggie closed her eyes and leaned her head heavily into his hand. "Do you want me to be here?"

"Yes." He spoke the word like a prayer.

"Then I'll be here."

"Good. When I get back, we'll..."

She opened her eyes, and the inquisition entranced him. "We'll what?" she whispered.

His conscience rumbled. This conversation should have started and ended with sex if it started at all. But when Jordon forced the crass words to his lips, he couldn't free them. Here was a man who made a living stating his demands. And suddenly, he didn't know what to ask for.

"Go. You're going to be late. When you get back we'll...talk." She didn't look certain of her words. And as she stared at him with shiny eyes, all he wanted was to bury himself inside of her.

"Okay." The word was weak, but it was stronger than his pulse. With the help of shallow breaths, he managed to walk out of the room without kissing her goodbye.

If he let his lips touch hers, he knew he'd never make his flight.

CHAPTER NINE

The dark sky opened with rain to spoil Maggie's day. This was a fresh insult, and she felt the foreign inclination to thumb her nose at the universe. For two weeks she'd enjoyed pleasant temperatures and sunny days. Jordon left and the sky darkened as if he were its power source.

Pushing her chest off a blanket spread on the living room floor, Maggie arched her back and held the posture while she faced the lake being beaten by rain. She missed him. A groan crossed her lips and she tried to clear her mind again, but she was too tormented. Her arms gave out, dumping her body to the floor.

"Dr. Maggie?"

"Just Maggie, Carlos. You don't need the doctor part." She didn't feel much like an expert anyway.

"Okay. Maggie, come see the washer. I think something's wrong. It's shaking."

She drew a breath, and her stomach and chest pushed against the hard floor. "You probably loaded it unevenly, but that's easy to fix."

Rolling onto her knees, she stood and turned her back on the yoga and the rain. She padded through the living room, passed through the kitchen and entered the laundry room with Carlos like a puppy on her heels. "Lift the lid."

"But it's running."

"It'll stop when you lift the lid."

He followed her directions.

"You have to spread sheets out like this." She reached into the belly of the metal beast and tugged at the twisted clothes. "See what I'm doing?"

He nodded.

"Good. Close her up and she should be a lot happier."

The machine purred to life, and Carlos's eyes widened in amazement. "Thanks."

They were long overdue for a talk. Maggie patted his shoulder. "Follow me, young man."

She led him to the dining room where she had placed a plastic container of supplies earlier that morning. The dark sky continued to cry and block the sunlight. Maggie flipped a switch and lit the iron chandelier hanging over the glass table. "Did you ever play with Play-Doh when you were little?"

His face went blank, and he shrugged. "No."

"Well, you're going to do it now." She held out a ball of blue modeling compound. "Go ahead. Touch it."

Carlos hesitated. "Why?"

"It's an exercise meant to get creative juices flowing." She held the ball closer to him. "Come on. Do it for me."

He pushed a finger deep into the ball. "Gross."

She laughed. "It is a little weird." Flattening the blue ball between her hands, she dropped the dough to the table where she poked twice at the top of the circle and once in a u-shape across the bottom. "Mr. Smiley."

Carlos looked at her like she'd lost her mind. Jordon looked at her like that too. Her stomach felt heavy, and she lifted her gaze to the misery outside. "Anyhow...I want you to make something for me."

"What?"

"I'd like you to make an image of yourself, something that represents you." She gestured to the only rainbow they were going to see today, lining the dining table. "You can use any color you'd like."

He hesitated again, but then lifted the plastic can of white. He studied the unblemished, snowball shape in his hand and then traded it for a clump of red, smashing it between his tan hands. Bushy black brows knitted together in concentration.

With a pinch here and a push there, he shaped the flattened clay into a big red heart. Smiling, he reached again for the white ball. He peeled a strip of red from the heart and smoothed the injured area before breaking off a tiny piece of red and rolling it between his thumb and forefinger. His trepid movements mesmerized her, and it only took one fleck of red placed on the ball of white for her to recognize a baseball.

When he finished, a grinning Carlos sat back and admired his work. "Like that?"

A heart and a baseball. Light infiltrated the clouds, and Maggie felt recharged. "Like that."

He grabbed for the blue ball and poked.

"If you didn't do stuff like this as a kid, what did you do?" she asked.

"Played baseball."

"Playing professional baseball means a lot in your country, doesn't it?"

"*Sí.*" He rolled the blue clay between his palms.

"Do any of your other siblings play baseball?"

He sniffed. "I have sisters."

"They must be very proud of you."

He stopped playing with the clay and something in his yellow eyes stirred her pain. "They need the money. My father died."

Another piece of the emotional puzzle snapped into place. "I can imagine how important the financial support is to them, but that's an awfully big burden on you. Do you mind supporting them?"

He looked to the microwave clock over Maggie's right shoulder. "No." He dropped the clay. "Time for *House Hunters.*" Pushing against the table, he stood without another word.

Maggie gave a weak smile and started stuffing balls of clay into their plastic containers. "I'll leave this stuff on the table in case you want to mess around with it later."

He didn't respond.

She was close to a breakthrough, but still so far away.

After cleaning and lingering a bit in case Carlos decided to talk more, Maggie thought it was safe to call Crystal. She was wrong.

"Moving to Idaho is a bad idea," Maggie warned.

"It sounds like you're disapproving of my right to be a free, unadulterated participant in this life. And that makes me wonder what's going on in North Carolina? You're closing up. I sense it all the way out here."

"I'm not closing. I'm navigating some confusing spots."

"Then let's talk, and we can pray for illumination."

Maggie didn't feel like praying. She felt like screaming at her thick-skulled mother, who thought traveling to Idaho with Paul and Katherine was a good idea.

"Magpie, tell me what's bothering you."

The spider appeared in her dreams again last night, and once again the eight-legged nemesis led her straight to Jordon. Was she supposed to save Jordon or was she supposed to save herself from Jordon? The pressure built in her head. As much as she wanted to focus on Crystal, to talk her out of further separating herself from mainstream society by becoming a polygamist, Maggie was struggling. Maybe Crystal could help.

"I'm having reoccurring dreams about a spider. The scenery changes slightly, but the spider is the same every night."

"The spider is symbolic of your power as a woman."

Maggie dipped the receiver from her mouth and scoffed. "Yep. That's the conclusion I originally came to." But after exerting her feminine power over Jordon in the backseat of his car and having the dreams continue… "I'm having second thoughts."

"Why? What does the spider do?"

"The spider teases me, urges me to follow it, and talks to me."

"What does the spider say?"

"Save me."

"Oh, Magpie. And you're worried about me?"

Uncomfortable weight imprisoned Maggie's chest as she tried to breathe. "Why? What's wrong?"

"You're the spider. You're the one who needs saving, but from what? You aren't telling me the whole story."

Of course she wasn't telling Crystal the whole story. Where would she start? At the beginning, when Maggie took an insane assignment across the country rather than stay home and navigate her nervous breakdown under Crystal's nose, or at the end, when Maggie couldn't bring herself to escape Jordon?

With a sigh, Maggie aimed to close the conversation. "There isn't anything to tell. Carlos is making progress, but I'm having a hard time getting to the point where that progress is tangible."

"You and your tangibility. Haven't I always told you what's touchable isn't what's most important?"

"You have."

"Then why do you insist on holding on to the physical world? Be free, darling. Be free to save yourself."

Maggie wallowed in confusion. If she was the spider who needed saving, how was she supposed to accomplish the feat? If Maggie wasn't the spider, then who was? An underused space of critical thinking roared to life in Maggie's brain. *Sometimes a dream is just a dream.* The voice in her head wasn't her voice—it was Jordon's.

It always came back to Jordon.

Maggie spent the next hour in bed with her laptop opened to real estate pages, while Carlos was locked in his room on the phone. If Crystal was serious about being with Paul and Katherine, Maggie wanted out of her mother's house as soon as possible. She was starting to realize even open-mindedness had its closing point. For Maggie, polygamy was apparently that point. She couldn't imagine her life intertwined with Crystal, Paul, and Katherine.

Closing her eyes, Maggie tried to visualize her dream home. She conjured an image of a stone walk, which led to a large white door. When she opened the door, Jordon was waiting for her, standing in front of the glass sliding doors. Sunlight bounced off the ever-blue lake, surrounding him in a halo.

She snapped her lids open and slammed her laptop shut.

Attachment was a dangerous game, but still, Maggie wished Jordon would call. No matter how much she lamented and analyzed the situation, one thing was clear. Carlos was the reason she came to North Carolina, but Jordon was the reason she stayed. What she wouldn't give to find him sitting on the pier, where they could explore their feelings and get the answers to all their questions— even if the answers pushed them apart. At least then she'd be sure. She hated being stuck between torment and indecision. Why was it so many of life's struggles rooted in relationships?

The simple, hypothetical question became a revelation, and her brain lightened. In her moment of clarity, Maggie would've bet her credentials that Carlos Nunez thought he was in love, and a woman stood between him and his successful return to the plate.

*

Jordon glanced at his watch as he stepped off the elevator, thinking again about calling Maggie. He had a couple hours between meetings and plenty of time to check on her progress with Carlos.

With a tug on his tie, he growled. Who was he kidding? He cared about Carlos's progress, but this time it was an excuse to call Maggie. Jordon wasn't an excuses kind of guy. Too bad he'd been making excuses where Maggie was concerned since the day they met.

Shoving through the revolving doors on a wave of disgust, Jordon filtered into the New York City crowd. He walked a few blocks, hoping to clear his head and gain some perspective. Instead, he came face to face with his ex-wife.

Bethany's rounded stomach stretched between the edges of her tweed coat, overshadowing her boobs. Jordon found an odd satisfaction in the fact that his favorite part of her body was no longer the main attraction.

"Oh, my God," she squealed, throwing her arms around his neck and pushing her belly into his side. "How are you?"

Jordon wrapped his hands around her wrists and unlatched her from his neck. "Busy."

She settled to her feet and spied him through narrowed eyes. "So nothing's changed?"

He stared at the bump that housed another man's child. "I'd say a lot has changed. Good luck with that." He made a gesture toward her stomach and stomped away.

The tapping behind him warned that she'd followed. Maybe he could out-walk her. After all, she was in heels, and with a belly like that, she couldn't have much balance.

Who wore heels when they were pregnant? Bethany, of course. He rolled his eyes.

"You know, I'd hoped we could be civil when we ran into each other like this."

Jordon chuckled and picked up his pace. She was an idiot.

"Jordon, please." She whined loudly enough to paint him the jerk who would upset a pregnant woman.

With his eyes closed, he stopped. "What more could you possibly want from me?"

When he opened his eyes, she was standing there, staring at him like he'd mutated into a wounded animal worthy of pity. "I never...I thought..." And then her cold blue eyes pooled with tears.

His stomach clawed into his throat. This wasn't happening. Jordon Kemmons wasn't standing in the middle of a busy Times Square sidewalk, facing his pregnant ex-wife. But he was, and he couldn't figure out how to make her go away. If he walked, and she caused a scene, word was bound to get around. And while the agent tried not to care about his reputation, the man was already struggling.

"I have a meeting in five," he lied, hoping the agent could end this conversation without personal drama.

But she stepped forward and tugged on his lapel. "I just wanted to say hello. I wanted to see how you were doing. I think about you."

He winced.

"I know you'll never believe this, but I want you to be happy." She raised her voice over honking horns.

He considered wincing again, but he was too numb to manage the expression.

Sliding a hand to her stomach, she smiled. It was a look he'd rarely seen. "God, Jordon, there is so much more to life than money and power."

Easy for her to say.

Dropping his face into his scarf to hide the dry heaves, Jordon spun around and walked away. He wasn't going to be subjected to another minute of her self-righteous attempt to mend his broken heart. His heart wasn't broken, he thought, clenching his fists inside his coat pockets. His ego was bruised, and his bank account was drained, but his heart was fine…he never gave it to her in the first place. And that had been their fatal mistake.

Obviously Bethany didn't make the same mistake twice. By the joyful look on her face despite his icy reception of her, it was clear she loved the asshole she cheated with. Not that love made what she'd done any better. But in a sick way it gave Jordon hope. If she could lie and cheat and still find happiness, then why couldn't he?

The low-lying fog gathering between skyscrapers began to clear, and Jordon allowed himself a moment of uncharacteristic spiritual belief. It was a sign. It had to be.

With his head high and his mind clear for the first time in years, Jordon faced the future. First, he would close this deal for Manuel, and then he would go home to Maggie.

CHAPTER TEN

Maggie managed some half-hearted yoga postures and meditated for a measly five minutes before her obsession with Carlos's love life forced her into a walk around the cul-de-sac. No matter what approach she took, Carlos managed to avoid the topic of romantic interests, further convincing her that a woman stood between him and a successful return to the plate.

Later in the evening, Maggie settled onto the sofa next to Carlos for another try at a confession. She succeeded at watching *House Hunters* and sharing miso soup and vegetarian spring rolls with him, but deep conversation failed.

As the days passed, Maggie spent the hours holding Skype sessions for other clients, cleaning the house and making excuses to be around Carlos. Eventually her stalking lead to Carlos dragging her onto the elliptical machine in Jordon's gym. He ran several miles to her walking one. As usual, *House Hunters International* blared from the flat screen.

"Do you have a girlfriend?" Maggie blurted the question out of desperation.

Carlos clenched his mouth shut, killed the motor on his machine and walked away.

By Thursday, Maggie admitted defeat. Carlos remained distant. Crystal remained unreachable. And Jordon remained in New York. She was growing more and more uncomfortable staying in North Carolina without him.

Friday blended into Saturday and then Sunday, with only Bernie's voice on the phone to break the monotony. "I'm coming to pick you two up. Boss Man wants you out of the house."

"Is that so?" Maggie struggled to keep her frustrations from spilling onto Bernie.

"Yes. He called to check on you."

A childish huff echoed into the phone. "Why doesn't he call me to check on me?"

"I don't know why you two do what you do. I'm just the messenger." Bernie's rich laughter wasn't enough to make her smile.

He arrived thirty minutes later and drove them to the Harris Teeter grocery store down the street. While Bernie waited in the car, Carlos pushed a shopping cart with his forearms, and Maggie loaded it.

"Did you talk to Jordon last night?" She didn't look at Carlos. She didn't want him to see how anxious she was for information.

"*Si.*"

"And?"

"He's happy I'm working out, and he says I throw when he gets home."

"When is he coming home?" She held an ice-cold carton of soy milk to her sweating chest.

Carlos shrugged.

She dropped the soy milk into the cart and stalked ahead. This was ridiculous. She was here for Carlos. Jordon didn't matter. He was never supposed to be in North Carolina in the first place. And she was never supposed to stay long enough for things to get complicated. This job was an opportunity for her to simplify her life and gain greater independence. If she was optimistic, a few conversations with Carlos was all that stood between her and a plane ride home. But if she was honest, something more than a few conversations with Carlos was keeping her here. She couldn't decide whether to be honest or optimistic.

If Maggie thought hearing from Jordon would make the choice easier, she was wrong.

"I'm sorry I didn't call sooner. I've been busy," he said in that skin-tingling voice she'd come to know.

Maggie leaned against her seagrass headboard, brushing the bumps from her arms with a reminder that he hadn't been too busy to call Bernie and Carlos. "It's no big deal," she spouted a little too enthusiastically.

"It is to me. I've been thinking about you...a lot...for a long time actually, and I wanted you to know."

She rubbed her knuckles against the knot between her breasts and told herself his words made matters worse. How was she supposed to simplify her life by indulging in a man who complicated everything? "Jordon, don't."

"Don't what?"

"Don't make this complicated."

He quieted long enough to make her squirm. "Maggie, I'm not complicating anything. From where I sit, it's pretty simple. I know what I want."

"Sex," she said matter-of-factly.

"For starters."

Her throat squeezed shut. Then what? After the sex, after Maggie left North Carolina, then what? Her brain refused to go there. Collins women didn't fall in love, and they most certainly didn't marry. Foolish notions and archaic institutions. Then she remembered where her mother was and what she might be doing. Marrying Paul and Katherine. But it wasn't the same. For starters, polygamy was illegal, and it wasn't recognized as normal by society. While those things were deterrents to Maggie, they attracted her mother. Leave it to Crystal to find a version of marriage that coincided with her spiritual beliefs. But what about Maggie?

"I gotta go. Carlos needs me," she lied. Karma would make her pay. But now more than ever, she needed to fix Carlos and leave... before she weakened enough to make a terrible mistake.

*

The next day, Maggie sunk into the deep cushions of the couch while Justin Guarini belted out Al Green's *Let's Stay Together* from the flat screen above the fireplace.

"Do you think we could talk about what happened in the lake?" she asked.

Carlos flinched and stared at the screen. "I'm sorry."

"You don't have to apologize. You were in pain. People in pain sometimes do things they wouldn't normally do. You're feeling better now, and that's what matters."

He nodded and pressed his lips together.

Another one-sided conversation, she thought. *Great*. And yet this time she couldn't back down. Jordon's phone call left her with a new sense of urgency.

Taking a breath in, Maggie gripped the amulet through her shirt. "Sometimes our emotions hold us prisoner. The way we feel about another person or the way another person feels about us can have a negative impact on our lives if we let it. Carlos, romantic love isn't..." She stopped before she gave her mother's abysmal version. "Romantic love is complicated and confusing."

He widened his eyes, and she had the distinct impression that she was getting through.

"Are you in love with Jordon?" he asked.

"No. No," she sputtered. "I wasn't talking about me. I was talking about you."

Every muscle in his face contorted before he hid the ugly reaction with a turn of his head. He dug his fingers into the arms of the chair with such force the gesture made Maggie's skin crawl. Watching his body contort, an ominous feeling replaced Maggie's excitement at breaking through. She tried to stomp the dread, but the more he tensed, the more she sensed some accuracy.

"Do *you* love Jordon?" she whispered.

He snapped his head around and stared at her. "No."

Maggie exhaled and allowed herself a small smile. "I'm sorry if I insulted you. I was going with my gut. I figured it was a girlfriend issue, but then I got this feeling, and you seemed so pained I thought... I'm sorry."

She didn't have time to pout at her inaccuracy, because Carlos shook his head slowly. "But I am...gay." He paled.

Maggie squared her shoulders and nodded. Suddenly, it all made perfect sense. "Okay," she said, smiling.

He shook his head again and blinked back tears.

Maggie swallowed hard, trying to choose a course of action, wishing she could celebrate the break through she'd been working for. But one thought of Jordon quelled her satisfaction. Could a man like Jordon Kemmons understand a man like Carlos Nunez?

As if the young man read her mind, he bit into his bottom lip. "Don't tell Jordon."

She sighed. "I can't. It's called patient-doctor confidentiality, and it's an important part of what I do."

The words seemed to relax Carlos, but they worried Maggie. Jordon expected answers, and this was a big one, maybe the reason a multi-million dollar player failed to live up to expectations.

"Beckett got traded," Carlos blurted, shoving the back of his hand across his runny nose. "Now I can't visit him. What if someone finds out?"

Maggie slid across the couch and rested a hand on his shoulder as he cried. She didn't follow sports. She hated the idea of men proving their worth by beating on each other. Even in baseball where contact wasn't part of every play, Maggie didn't understand the allure. Men with big sticks, swinging at balls and running around a bunch of bags—it wasn't quantum physics. They weren't feeding the hungry. They weren't saving souls. Still, Maggie understood one thing: pro sports and homosexuality didn't mix. One definitely threatened the macho image of the other.

She slipped an arm around Carlos's shoulder. "Does your family know you're gay?"

He hung his head. "No. They can never know. Never. No one can know, but you. Please, Maggie."

She gulped. "You have my word."

By sunset, Maggie's nerves were shot. The only thing keeping her calm was the entrancing motion of the rocking pier. She thought about leaving and continuing treatment virtually, but a revelation like Carlos's couldn't be taken lightly. If she left him now, he could misconstrue her departure and plunge into despair.

Then there was Crystal. Maggie hadn't spoken to her mother for over a week, and she wasn't sure she wanted to. Even though Maggie was desperate for information about the Idaho trip, she was going to have to prioritize the souls she saved. Crystal was an adult, and for the time being, Crystal was going to have to take care of herself. Maggie had enough to take care of around here.

Carlos slept peacefully after Maggie assured him for the thousandth time that she wouldn't reveal his secret. Sitting on the end of the pier, struggling to warm herself against the chilly wind, Maggie wondered if she'd ever sleep peacefully again. Panic blocked the air to her chest, and she opened her mouth to breath. She was tired of saving other people. Worse yet, she didn't know how to save herself. Lifting her face to the starry sky, she prayed for a savior.

*

Jordon owned houses in New York City, Tampa and Lake Norman, but the only one he cared about was this one...because Maggie was here. In five years of marriage, he never rushed home to Bethany. Then again, Bethany stopped being at home shortly after the wedding: "Why should I wait around for you to come to me?" Seeing her brought back all the ugly words, and they hurt.

Jordon didn't want to hurt anymore.

Besides, he had reason to celebrate. All anybody had to do was turn on twenty-four hour sports television to learn that

Jordon Kemmons was once again "the man." Manuel deserved the pay raise, and Jordon deserved the cut. It took guts to go in with outlandish demands. It took bigger guts to expect results from those demands. Jordon knew the people around that table thought he was crazy, but he didn't care. Negotiating an eight-year, one-hundred-and-eighty-million-dollar contract gave a man confidence enough to wear crazy like a Valentino suit.

Jordon dropped his leather bag in the darkened foyer and headed up the stairs. Carlos's door was closed as usual, but last night, the kid had sounded good on the phone. Hope surged in Jordon as he recalled Carlos talking about conditioning. Maggie deserved praise for the progress, and Jordon fully intended to praise her…all night long.

The thought painted a lusty smile on his face. He'd been waiting for her, for this. He only hoped the reality would live up to his expectations.

Spying Maggie's bedroom door ajar, Jordon loosened his tie. A few steps more and he stood in the darkened room. Blankets gathered at the end of the empty bed. No light spilled from the bath. He tensed. Glancing at the dresser, he caught the glimmer of her jewelry in the moonlight, and he filled with relief. Of course she wasn't gone. He gave his head a self-deprecating shake.

Back on the loft, Jordon stopped to stare out the picture windows. It was too black to see much more than flickering lights on the water, but his gut told him she was there. He raced through the house, his pounding heart his guide. He'd been away from her long enough to know the separation didn't make him happy. Which was ironic, since he hadn't been away long enough to forget how tumultuous their interactions could be. It didn't make sense, but he was tired of analyzing it. He was done fighting whatever supreme power got a sadistic kick out of pushing them together.

When he finally settled his eyes over her body sitting on the end of the pier, the shadowy sight sent electricity shooting through him like bolts of heat lightning.

She swung around on her bottom with a startled look on her face. "You're home."

Jordon felt flu-ish, his head spinning, his muscles weakening, his temperature soaring. "I am."

"Was your week…productive?"

"You could say that." He didn't want to brag. Besides, contracts and dollar amounts couldn't keep him warm at night. He unbuttoned his suit coat and let it slip off his shoulders. "Aren't you cold?" He couldn't stop his gaze from dipping to chest level, looking for the answer beneath her plain white T-shirt.

She pulled her knees to her chest, blocking his view. "No. I'm fine. Listen, Jordon. A lot has happened this week. It was… productive."

He figured the shock on her face and the tripping over her words had something to do with his unannounced arrival. He should've been clear about his return, and he planned to apologize for his facetious behavior. Later.

Jordon stood over her, tugging his shirt tails from his dress pants. "Carlos told me he's working out, and all his laundry's clean. Thank you."

Her shoulders dropped as she released a breath, and her eyes twinkled in the darkness like tractor beams of energy, pulling him to his knees. He leaned in for a kiss.

Maggie leaned back. "Why is it you call him every night, but you rarely call me?"

All right. Maybe he'd apologize now. He smiled. "I'm sorry. I thought about calling you a lot more than I did, but I needed to concentrate on the negotiations. I think about you enough without talking to you. I just needed some space." He attempted to kiss her again, and she pulled back even more, bracing her weight on her palms.

"Then I can give you space."

He inched closer. "I don't want any more space."

"Then we can talk."

"I don't want to talk." He unfastened the buttons of his shirt, the cat-and-mouse game stirring his desire. "I want you."

A little sound escaped her mouth a second before his lips covered hers.

Jordon figured this could go one of two ways. Either he had a hell of a lot of convincing to do, or Maggie missed him as much as he missed her.

She kissed him back, which was a good sign, and he lifted a hand to the side of her neck, deepening the kiss. When her fingers grazed his bare chest, he crumbled, crawling into her until her body flattened against the pier.

Her tongue mixed with his in a mysterious rhythm he couldn't imagine replicating with anyone else: light swirls, firm sweeps and desperate plunges, flooding his throat with lust and making his body ache for more. He held the back of her head, pushing deeper into her mouth.

For a moment, he rested on top of her, filling with need, but the heat and friction of her body threatened his resolve. He slipped to her side and settled on the pier, their mouths still tangled.

With one arm cradling her head, he ran the other hand down the top of her chest, stopping to explore her breasts. Seventeen again with shaky hands and shallow breaths, Jordon fumbled through the motions. But then Maggie smoothed her hand over his zipper, and the gentle pressure nearly sent him off the pier to douse the flames.

Slow down. The words roared in his head. He grabbed her hand and pressed it to her stomach. "Keep your hands to yourself. It's my turn."

"Okay." She sounded distant, and he hoped it had something to do with the hem of her shirt being lifted over the smooth skin of her stomach and his mouth dipping to her navel. If there was another reason, one that meant she was having second thoughts, he didn't want to know. But if there were doubts, he'd be damn sure to erase them.

Jordon circled his tongue and lapped at the shallow hole of velvet. He smiled against her belly when she arched her lower back in search of more pleasure. All too happy to oblige, he ran his tongue higher along her stomach, pushing the fabric over her breasts.

The moonlight blanketed her body in beautiful shadows, and he recognized the silhouette of his face floating on her milky skin as if she were branded…as if she were his. Lightheadedness returned, and he had to remind himself to breath before he passed out.

He couldn't remember feeling so much torment. Covering her breast with his mouth, he slid his tongue around the hardened skin and then wrapped both arms underneath her arching back, drawing her body deeper into his, sucking the light out of her, directing it straight into the blackest parts of him.

She gasped and held his head to her heart. In that moment, he wished she'd never let him go.

Brushing his lips across the breast he'd worshipped, he turned to the other, but before he ravaged the sensitive mound, words spilled into the silent night. "You're mine, Maggie. I claim you."

He sucked her into his mouth and into his soul.

*

Maggie opened her passion-weary eyes and tried to calm her breathing by focusing on the stars. But there was nothing she could do to stop it now. This wasn't salvation. This was possession.

Crystal's words barged into Maggie's head: *Love is a word we use to describe an obsessive need to possess. And possession leads to loss and loss leads to pain.*

Maggie knew a moment of terror, but then a tremor of pleasure rocked her body so soundly she expected the heavens to open and swallow her whole. This was sex. This wasn't love. There was no need for panic. With an ache for him building in her core, she managed a weak promise to keep perspective.

Jordon released her, and chilly wind rushed across her wet chest as he pushed to sit. She burned for him. And when his eyes locked with hers before they roved over her body, she saw such tenderness her promise shattered.

"Take off your shirt."

Maggie obeyed, despite nagging reminders that she received too much and gave too little.

He ran a hand down the curve of her shoulder and then gripped her neck with his other hand, pulling her in for a deep, draining kiss. She slipped a hand beneath the open edge of his dress shirt, anxious to give more than she received.

"Not yet," he said, snatching her hand and holding it to his heart. "I want you to stand first."

She held onto him as she stood on the rocking pier. He kneeled and her heart swelled with understanding. This beautiful, powerful man wanted to spend tonight giving pleasure to her.

He curled his fingers around the waist of her yoga pants, dragging them down. A cold breeze blew, but she filled with unearthly warmth. He slipped his hands over the curves of her backside and tilted his reverent face to hers before rubbing his lips below her naval and drawing his mouth lower.

Nerve endings exploded when his tongue pressed between her folds. The intensity made her hold on to him for more than balance. If she fell, she would plunge off the pier into the murky depths. She suspected the thought was a warning, but the sexy jolts piercing her body banished further reason.

He took the flesh between her legs with the same intensity as he took her breasts, drawing every last ounce of magic from the smallest points of pleasure. Sucking. Tugging. Pulling. Teasing. And then licking with a laziness that made her lose control. A violent rush carried her cries into the night.

Jordon wrapped his hands around her wrists and pulled her down. They tumbled together, sprawling across the pier with Maggie falling on top of him. She welcomed the collapse, the protection of his arms and the blanket of ecstasy. With her nose buried in his evergreen-scented neck, she slowly returned to her surroundings. The pier rocked gently on the waves while the November wind blew lightly over her goose-pimpled skin. Jordon's fingertips traced her back, slipping over her curves. She smoothed her cheek against his and lowered her lips to his mouth. He smelled like a man and tasted like a lover.

When he opened for her, her tongue barely touched his before his arms tightened around her waist. "Now it's your turn, Maggie."

She pulled back and stared at the shadows on his face. She didn't see an ounce of darkness, only deep desire. His lids were heavy, and his tongue slipped back and forth over his bottom lip.

"But go easy on me," he said with a smile.

She pushed to straddle his thighs and reached for his belt buckle. While she unbuttoned his pants and loosened the zipper, he remained still except for his eyes. They followed every move.

"Can you at least lift your butt?" she teased, gripping the waist bands of his pants and boxers.

He chuckled as she slid the clothes down his legs and crawled over him to nip his lips.

"I don't know what it is about you, but I like relinquishing control," he said in a whisper against her lips. "Just don't go around telling anyone. I have a rep to protect."

Another secret to keep. Only this one Maggie didn't mind keeping. And the other one...she wouldn't have to keep forever. She'd help everyone get what they needed, starting with Jordon.

Maggie dragged her lower half over his erection as she kissed him. He didn't kiss her back. His hands stayed at his side. Apparently, he was serious about submitting.

She laughed against his mouth. "Oh, I see how you are. You want me to do all the *dirty* work."

"Exactly." His perfect smile glowed in the moonlight. "Reach into my coat pocket."

She straightened, ran her hands over his hardened length and twisted toward the discarded pile of clothes, searching until she found a box stuffed inside his pocket.

"I came prepared," he said.

Straddling his thighs again, Maggie worked his penis with her hands. "You brought an entire box. You're awfully confident this is going to become a habit." She threw him her best smoldering look as she rolled a condom into place. "But I'm not convinced," she added, moving to hover above his erection.

Without warning, Jordon gripped her waist and thrust inside of her. "How about now?"

She needed a second to recover from the unexpected jolt and the fact that Jordon wasn't a complete pushover. Of course he wasn't. He was only rusty, probably hoping the Maggie-on-top position guaranteed success. And why, oh why was she analyzing the first meaningful sex she'd had in years?

Drawing a couple deep breaths, she refocused and let the feel of him inside of her radiate through her body. Only then did she move.

He watched, his hands sliding over her thighs.

Emotions grew from the place where they connected and built in intensity as they climbed her belly, swirled around her heart and whimpered out through her open mouth. So much power. So much pleasure. She was giving, but she was receiving, too. Had she ever done both simultaneously?

Maggie smiled and dragged the tip of her tongue across the ends of her upper teeth. "This could become a habit." Her hands slipped over her breasts as she rocked against him.

He moaned. "Absolutely."

Jordon smoothed his palms over the tops of Maggie's thighs until his fingers reached the slick between her legs. The added pleasure made her rhythm as erratic as her breathing, and she leaned forward, bracing her arms on the wood beside his head. He grabbed hold of her bottom and pumped harder, forcing her out of control, out of her body, fighting to stay present.

Colossal pressure built above their joining and clawed across her skin until it exploded in her head. Jordon breathed her name and drew her to his chest, shuddering and gasping for air in her ear. Heat molded their bodies beneath the stars.

Maggie wasn't in love. She wasn't saved. But she was certainly satisfied.

CHAPTER ELEVEN

Maggie pushed off the pier and plunged head first into the dark water. Cold liquid bit her skin, sending a crash-cart shock to recharge her soul.

"What the hell are you doing? That water's barely sixty degrees." Jordon's voice penetrated the water as she surfaced.

"I needed a jolt," she said, slicking back her hair. "It's symbolic."

He sat naked on the pier except for his open dress shirt, his legs dangling in the water. "I'll give you a jolt. I negotiated an eight-year, one-hundred-and-eighty-million-dollar contract."

The numbers strung together in her head. "That's a lot of money."

"I know."

She could see his smile, and the joy drew her to him. Cutting through the crisp water with such peace, she wrapped her arms around his legs and stared at his face.

"It's a lot of money, and it's all over the news, but you know what I was thinking about the minute those papers were signed? Actually, even before those papers were signed?"

"What?" She ran wet hands ran along his strong calf muscles.

"You. And I never let my personal life mix with my business life." He threw his hands into the air. "I'm not sure what to make of that."

Neither was she. Holding his feet and letting her body float on the water, she lifted her face to the sky. "I think you're entitled to be obsessed with sex since you've been holding back for a while. It's normal to become rather compulsive when you're deprived of something. The desire will fade."

"You make it sound so clinical."

"Because it is." Something inside of her ruptured, and sadness bubbled in her chest.

"But what if there's more to it?"

Detach. Her body sunk, as she let go of him, and she treaded water to keep from going under. There was a point in every relationship where the potential for attachment pushed Maggie away. She hoped the point wasn't now—not so soon after feeling so wonderful.

She thrashed her arms and legs below the surface. "What more could there be?"

"Maggie, what if we're meant to be together?"

Water slipped into her open mouth and she choked. When her coughs quieted, she tried her best to rationalize his words. "That's impossible. We're complete opposites. You think I'm a flake, remember?"

"That was before I understood you. Now I think you're brilliant. You took the biggest flake of all…" he slapped a hand to his chest "…and you helped him work through some major stuff. I haven't felt this good in years."

Maggie started to sink again. When clients achieved relief from their troubles and opened their minds to the experiences of their early lives, they connected with their therapists, saw familiarity in their trusted confidantes. The phenomenon was called transference. And sometimes people confused the feeling with romantic love. Jordon wasn't her client, but she was helping him break through an intimacy drought, and she was helping him with Carlos. The line blurred.

As Maggie kicked harder to keep her head above the cold water, her teeth chattered. A therapist never created transference on purpose. It was a dangerous and powerful thing. Had she done it unknowingly with Jordon?

Her silence must have unnerved him, because he studied her with a wrinkled face. "What if I love you?"

She struggled to downplay his emotions. "Of course you love me. Love is the predominant feeling we should have for all human beings. You're thankful, feeling particularly favorable toward me, and you're confusing that for society's molested version of love."

"So I'm confused and molested?" He straightened and started buttoning his shirt. "How'd you ever get past your negative opinions long enough to screw me?" He reached for his pants. "Never mind. I get it. I can give you an orgasm, but I can't give you a future." He shoved his legs into his pants. "And here I thought I was the one who needed help."

Panic mixed with Maggie's full-body chill. "Don't go," she pushed the words past chattering teeth. "Let's talk about this."

He looked unbelievably wonderful, drenched in moonlight, with his shirttails blowing in the wind. She felt possessive, fearful, chilled to the bone and strangely aroused by the heightened emotions.

"If you want to talk, get out of the water. I feel like an idiot professing unrequited love to some mythical creature. I bet you have a tail. You probably spend half your life swimming the oceans causing perfectly sane sailors to lose their minds."

He'd come undone, babbling about mermaids in the moonlight, shoving his hands through his glorious black hair, and she'd done this to him, pushed him to the point of no control. There was something vulnerable and beautiful about the process. Her troubled mind raced for reason with a reminder that detachment was the smart thing to do.

Maggie didn't listen. Floating again, she lifted one leg out of the water and ran her hands down the length of skin. "See? No tail."

After a few silent seconds, his shirt floated to the pier and his body splashed into the lake.

He surfaced with his arms around her waist. "It's cold." He sounded miserable.

"It's refreshing." She wiped the water from his eyes and smoothed back his dripping hair.

The moonlight accentuated the painful shadows on his face. "Have you ever been in love, Maggie?"

She wasn't one to shy away from heavy conversations, but pressed against his naked body, she felt particularly defenseless. "I love almost everyone I meet," she said, hoping the teaching from her childhood would offer protection.

The wrinkles on his forehead deepened. "That's not what I meant."

She knew what he meant, and he deserved an honest answer, but these were the intricacies about her that would keep them apart. And she wasn't sure she was ready for that. Still, if they were destined to be apart, wasn't it better sooner than later?

The stabbing in her heart wasn't convincing. "No. I've never been in love." *Because romantic love doesn't exist.* She stopped before the worst part came out. He looked forlorn enough, like he waited on an answer he didn't entirely want to hear. Every part of his gorgeous face frowned. His eyes drooped. His cheeks caved. His lips sagged. She did the only thing she could think to do. She redirected the conversation back at him. "Did you love your ex-wife?"

"I guess not, not if the marriage ended the way it did. I used to think love was about the perks, the hot wife, the huge house, the sex I was entitled to. It was disgusting and immature. And I paid for it."

Maggie smoothed a wrinkle from his cheek. "And now, what do you think love is about?" The question came out of a need to know from someone other than her mother.

Jordon spun her around in the water. "Love is about being happy." He let go of her, plunging under the water and disappearing.

Maggie tipped her head to the sky for guidance. She wanted to believe in an unselfish, prolonged state of attraction that filled a person's body and soul with joy, but she knew better. She knew a rush of subjective emotions lurked behind the romantic notion. And she knew emotions were fleeting.

But what if she was wrong? What if she could love a man for no other reason than because it made her happy? No enlightenment. No threat to her spiritual experience. If she could love like that, would it be Jordon? They were from opposite sides of the country and opposite sides of the spirituality spectrum. Their only commonalities were lust and a troubled young man. Was it enough? Carlos wouldn't always be troubled, and lust would wane.

Maggie shivered. Jordon didn't love her. He didn't know her. He'd never seen her walk barefoot over embers. He'd never met her mother. A mainstream man like Jordon would run from Maggie's circus sideshow life.

Jordon's shadowy head appeared further out in the lake. "Maggie, I don't care what you say, *I* say I'm falling in love with you."

Once again, thoughts of transference clogged her throat. It was the best explanation of how they went from a strange and strong attraction to talking about love. If it was transference, her carelessness was unforgiveable, and she had to make it right.

"Jordon, you aren't in love with me. You just think you are." She couldn't help herself; something pulled her from the safety of the pier, toward him. As she cut into the deeper water, her body grew colder.

He disappeared again, and her heart thudded in her chest. She spun around, searching the pitch black. The water nipping at her numbing skin left her senses compromised. She could see the dim lights of the house, but she wasn't sure how far she'd swum. *Save me.*

A rush of dread threatened to drag her under. "Jordon!"

He gripped her leg before he surfaced and pulled her into his arms.

She breathed through the pounding of her heart. "Don't do that again."

"Don't do what?"

"Disappear."

"I'm not going anywhere," he said with a grin. "The sex is way too good."

He tightened his grip and dragged them both under.

*

For the first time in weeks, Maggie didn't dream about spiders. In fact, she slept like she ate a poisoned apple, and when she woke, a shirtless Jordon sat at the end of the bed.

"You don't eat meat." He placed a bowl of fresh fruit on her comforter-covered belly.

She tried to decide whether he was being facetious. After all, before she climbed into his bed she refused to have sex with him again until they set some boundaries. It seemed rational at the time. With her confliction and his confession, Maggie wanted their next encounter to be deliberate. Between gentle kisses and heavenly full body hugs, Jordon tried to convince her that being together was a good idea, but Maggie fell asleep before she could agree.

She woke with a head no clearer than the night before and a body addicted to his touch. If Jordon was half as sexually frustrated as she was, eating meat most certainly had a double meaning. She raised her brows in question.

"What do you eat on Thanksgiving Day?" he clarified.

She poked the fork into a piece of mango and slipped it over her lips before speaking around the passion fruit. "I don't celebrate Thanksgiving."

"What?" He snagged a red grape out of her bowl and popped it into his mouth.

"I haven't celebrated a major holiday since I was in elementary school." She bit into another forkful. "Crystal thinks any holiday not tied to the cycle of the moon is an advertising ploy or a religious brainwashing and therefore not worthy of celebration."

"No stuffing? No cranberry salad?" His eyes bugged. "No Christmas? Didn't Santa come to your house?"

Maggie chewed and swallowed. "Nope. I wasn't allowed to participate in the rape of consumers and the division of the populous."

He shook his head. "God, you were deprived. I'm surprised you weren't homeschooled."

"Crystal said having a freethinking soul in the bowels of society's stronghold on the youth movement was much too valuable an opportunity to miss."

He took her empty bowl, placed it on the bedside table, and ran his hand along her arm. Her skin reacted like the addict it had become, rising to meet him, trembling at the prospect of more.

He brightened, his eyes sparkling in the morning sun. "Did you start many revolutions?"

"None. I couldn't get anyone to listen to me. They all thought I was strange," she said, savoring the tiny tickles his hand left behind.

He bent down and smacked a kiss to her lips. "Then it's settled. I was going to insist you go home to be with Crystal for Thanksgiving, but after hearing this, you're staying with me."

An odd rush of excitement swelled at the idea, but then the doubt that plagued her off and on all night resurfaced.

This isn't a game, Maggie. If you're not careful, if you don't maintain distance, someone's going to get hurt.

She smiled despite the frown in her heart. "I'm sure you'd rather spend the holidays with your family."

He lifted a shoulder. "I am my family. My mother died, and I don't speak to the rest of them."

Ouch. Professionally, Maggie understood the deep scars of family derision. Personally, she stood on the precipice many times. She knew how strong a person had to be to make difficult relationships work. "Why don't you talk to them?"

He turned to face the sunrise. "I don't want to talk about it. I want to shower." He stood and headed across the room. "And I want you to join me."

She watched the muscles of his body contract with each step until he disappeared into the master bath. She could make him tell her. All it would take would be a simple reminder. *If you love me, you would tell me.* But he didn't love her, and she never used emotion as leverage. Of course, that was the therapist speaking, the same therapist who chided her for being in Jordon's bed. The professional voice taunted her. *Why don't you look for perspective in your own bed? With all the questions crowding your mind, why are you still in his?*

Sighing, Maggie stared into the sun until her vision grew splotchy. As irrational as it seemed, she was here because she wanted to be. Even more irrational, she wished to be struck by a bolt of lightning and left with indisputable truth: *He loves you. Now, love him back.* And yet, if that happened, she'd be no better off, because she still wouldn't know how to be in love.

Maggie struggled with the voices in her head until water hissed from the bathroom pipes in the wall behind her head. Jordon was waiting. She had a choice to make. She could stay and analyze like a good therapist, or she could get up and join him like a woman gone mad with lust.

Tossing the covers off her naked body, Maggie stepped into the sun.

*

Jordon lathered his hair and stood under the spray of hot water. He figured she would join him eventually. Maggie might not be willing to admit that falling in love with him was a possibility, but he knew she felt a powerful pull. All that resisting, and yet the moment they touched her eyes rolled back and her lips parted to draw in more air. He felt it, too. It was like gravity, holding them together even when they wanted to be apart.

When he opened his eyes he saw her through the clear glass, standing outside the shower watching him, and his heart raced all over again. His gaze travelled her bare body, and the breath caught in his throat. She was strong, lean, bright, and flawless. While he'd never been a small breast kind of guy, his hands twitched and his mouth watered. Maggie changed his mind about a lot of things.

She pulled on the glass door and stepped into the streaming water. Watching her open her mouth to the spray made him hard. He grabbed her wrist, tugging her closer, wanting to give her the world. He'd start with sharing the Thanksgiving holiday, which was appropriate, because he'd never been more thankful than he was right now. Wouldn't the world be surprised to find out there was hope for Jordon Kemmon's cold heart?

He followed drops of water as they slid off her long lashes. She didn't believe he could love her, and, frankly, the revelation came as a shock to him, too. Neither one of them seemed like the loving type. He was too busy. She was too...opposed to the notion. He wasn't exactly sure what her hang-up was, but he figured enough sex and enough time together would change her mind. The sex wouldn't be a problem, but the time could be.

Jordon would have to work as hard on this relationship as he did on his career. A couple years ago he would've kicked his own ass for thinking such a stupid thing. But now? Now things felt different, and while he couldn't be with Maggie all of the time, he could make sure their time together mattered.

He took a deep breath. "I don't talk to my family, because… well…I was drafted in the first round, right out of high school. I'm backtracking here. Bear with me." He smiled and flicked his thumbs across her upper arms. "My father represented me during the draft, because he didn't want to give anyone else a cut. He ignored my requests to make college part of the contractual equation, and instead went for a bigger signing bonus."

She flattened a hand on his cheek, and the gesture encouraged Jordon to continue with a story he hadn't told in years.

"Dad disappeared after the first payout. He took the money and ran. I could've fought it legally, but I was shocked…and confused. I had all sorts of advice from all sorts of people, and what it came down to was that I'd been swindled by my own father, and I was stuck living inside his dream." The muscle in his cheek twitched, and he didn't try to hide the anger.

"Wasn't baseball your dream, too?" She traced the line of his jaw with her other hand and where she touched, he softened.

"I lost my entire childhood to baseball. I spent more hours on the couch with ice on my arm or traveling to games than I did playing with friends. My father was determined to make his sons professional athletes. I was standing on first base in Omaha when I realized what I wanted more than anything else was to go to law school and advocate for kids like me. So I quit."

Her hands stilled. "You quit baseball?"

"I went to college and then law school. I don't have a single regret." He didn't think she bought it.

Maggie dropped her hands to his pecs and her eyes narrowed. "Did you ever see your father again?"

This time, the muscles in both his cheeks pulsed, and he had to run his hands over her wet back to keep his fists from clenching. "Only on television during a news story about how he negotiated a contract for my brother straight out of high school."

"No."

"Yes. And I'd spent six months trying to guide Grey where pro ball was concerned, only to have him throw my advice away to be cheated by my dad."

"He cheated your brother, too?"

"Once a cheater, always a cheater, but I don't know for sure. I haven't heard details. People know not to talk to me about it. Sometimes a reporter will start with the questions, but those guys don't live long, and they serve as a reminder to the rest." Jordon let a lazy smile cross his lips, and he slipped one hand around her waist to play with her breast.

"You're not scary."

"Not now, but I am when I want to be, and that's the way I like it. The world I work in can't see weakness." Jordon reached for the body wash with his other hand and squirted a puddle into his palm. He wasn't going to let his father ruin anything else. Maggie got what she wanted. Now it was Jordon's turn.

Rubbing his palms together, he spread the soap over her shoulders and across her breasts. "See what happens when I show a little weakness?"

"What happens?" She wrapped her hands around his penis and pulled.

"People take advantage of me."

At the moment, he wasn't complaining.

CHAPTER TWELVE

Maggie was definitely taking advantage of Jordon, and she spent the better part of the day worrying about it. She knew he didn't mean his comment in the shower to be anything other than sexual banter, because he didn't know what she knew. He didn't know romantic love was a myth. He didn't know the power of transference. And he didn't know the truth about Carlos.

"I feel sick inside." Maggie cringed at the sight of a fish hanging off the end of Carlos's line. "How can you do that?"

He shrugged. "Help me let it go."

Maggie wrinkled every possible crease on her face and zipped her sweatshirt against the cold air. "I'm not touching it."

"Then I guess he'll have to eat it."

She turned toward the silky voice that had been stuck on a conference call for the last few hours. "Hardy, har, har."

"Here." Jordon pinched the line and pulled it toward him. He gripped the small catfish behind the head with his free hand and twisted the hook from the creature's mouth before he tossed it back into the lake. "See, no drama."

"Easy for you to say. You weren't hooked. I bet the fish was screaming on the inside." Maggie felt grumpy—grumpy about the fish and grumpy about her reaction to seeing Jordon. The mere sight of him had her heart palpitating. Seriously, she wondered if she might be destined for a complete physical and mental breakdown. Her moods dove, then climbed. Her body froze, then boiled. And her thoughts rode the same crazy waves.

Jordon took a step toward her with his fishy hands in front. "Is that what happens when you're hooked? You scream on the inside?" His lips curled.

She backed away. "Don't touch me with those hands."

He lunged for her, wrapping his arms around her waist as her right heel dipped off the back edge of the pier. She hadn't realized how close she was to falling.

"Now what do you think about my fishy hands?" Jordon asked, laughing. "Good catch, huh?"

Smiling with relief, she threw her arms around his neck and rested her chin on his shoulder. When she opened her eyes, she came face to face with a stunned Carlos. It didn't take long for the reason to register. The closer she got to Jordon, the more chances there were for her to spill Carlos's desperate secret.

Before Maggie could think of something comforting to say, Carlos moved further down the pier. "I'm going home."

Jordon released her and spun around to face Carlos. "That's great news, buddy. I'll have a ticket purchased. When do you want to leave?"

"I have a ticket. I leave after Thanksgiving and come back after New Year's."

A strange feeling crawled across Maggie's skin, and for some reason she wondered if Carlos was telling the truth. As she studied his somber face, another worry weighed on her mind. What would Carlos's departure mean for her and Jordon? With Carlos gone, her job was done.

Jordon didn't seem bothered by the same thoughts and feelings. He brightened and smacked Carlos on the back. "We got a lot of work to do before you leave. It's a good thing I called Petey."

Carlos nodded and, guided by Jordon's strong arm around his shoulders, moved toward the house. Maggie couldn't help but notice the sad shuffle of the young man's feet.

A couple hours later, she understood why. Petey was the pitching coach for Carlos's team, and there was nothing quite as eerie as an empty major league baseball stadium in the middle of November.

Carlos stood on the white rubber atop the pitching mound. He took so many deep breaths his shoulders looked like they were bobbing on ocean waves. He drew his arms over his head and kicked his knee high in front of him before he rocketed the ball toward home plate in one blurry motion.

Jordon nearly broke his neck leaping over the front row of seats behind home plate. "Ninety-seven. Sweet Jesus!" He spun around and climbed the two rows he jumped down. "Maggie, you're brilliant."

He kissed her. On the lips. In front of a handful of staffers and a gaping Carlos. Then he jumped down again and headed onto the field.

According to their contract, Maggie's purse just got a little fatter. She had the money she needed for her own place and an independent life, but she didn't feel a twinge of happiness. Carlos pitching faster solved nothing. He was still confused and heartbroken, and Jordon and Maggie were still playing a dangerous game, acting as if they had a future together despite the fact that Maggie knew better. She dropped her heavy head into her hands and listened to Jordon praise another pitch.

She needed to untangle from Jordon's arms, but she didn't have enough energy for multiple battles. Carlos had to come first. She'd get him to a place where he understood the magnitude of the situation facing him, where he could make decisions based on solid planning rather than emotion—which was a difficult feat for anyone let alone an impressionable twenty-year-old—and then she'd worry about detaching from Jordon.

Another lightning pitch whizzed toward the crouching catcher. Carlos stumbled off the mound as the small group gathering near the dugout talked with animation. Everyone celebrated his progress, everyone but him. He kicked his cleat into the dirt at the base of the mound and wandered around the perimeter with slumped shoulders and no direction.

Maggie's heart ached. She imagined a world where being gay didn't matter and she saw a different Carlos, a smiling, joyful Carlos. But in a world like that, Carlos wouldn't have slumped in the first place, and Maggie would've never come to Carolina…to Jordon.

She slapped her cheeks and separated from the scene. This wasn't about her, except for how Dr. Maggie Collins was going to guide a talented athlete in the face of pretty insurmountable odds. On one hand, if she encouraged him to embrace his sexuality, she could be setting him up for failure on the field. On the other hand, if she encouraged him to choose baseball, he faced a lifetime of conflict, defending or hiding his true self. As usual, she didn't have the answers.

Mother Goddess, help me. Maggie's phone rang before she could absorb the universe's reply.

"I'm getting married."

At the sound of Crystal's voice and ludicrous announcement, Maggie's head roared with pain. "What do you mean you're getting married?"

"I mean exactly what I said. Isn't it amazing, Magpie?"

"To Paul and Katherine?" Maggie took the stadium steps two at a time as she climbed higher off the field.

"Why do you insist on making everything I say about Paul and Katherine? I'm honestly worried about your narrowing."

"My narrowing?"

"Never mind. Magpie, it's Paul's father's farm, and you should see this place…"

Maggie didn't want to see anything other than her mother's feet on the ground—in Utah. Entering into a polygamist marriage crossed a line Maggie didn't know she'd drawn. Crazy crap was common place with Crystal, but this…this threatened…

What, Maggie? What did this threaten? Why was this different than any other alternative ideal?

Maggie couldn't open enough to think straight. She kept bumping into images of traditional families. Thanksgiving dinners. Kids. Grandkids. Fathers. Mothers. The fairy tale she didn't realize she kept stashed in her heart crowded everything else in her brain. Maggie struggled to stuff it back where it belonged, back where it couldn't disappoint or cause pain ever again. How could she think about a normal life if her holiday table included her mother, her mother's husband, and her mother's husband's wife?

Once a flake, always a flake.

Maggie's head spun, and she tripped on the top step. "I've got to go, *Mom*." It was a childish attempt at rebellion.

Crystal's breathing echoed. "What did you call me?"

Maggie opened her mouth to apologize, but then she balked at the ridiculous notion. She wasn't sorry. Crystal was her mom, whether she liked it or not. Maggie couldn't see a reason to hold back the truth. "I always wanted to call you mom."

"Darling, it's a word. The symbolism isn't positive once you strip back the layers."

Maggie pressed her knuckles to her forehead, hoping her hand might absorb some of the pain. "This isn't about what I call you. This is about you making selfish decisions that hurt the people around you."

Crystal gasped. "I can't deal with your negativity right now. I called to share good news, and you're depressing me. What's happened to you?"

The tips of Jordon's black and gray running shoes appeared in Maggie's peripheral vision, and she hung up. No good bye. She ended the call because she couldn't answer her mother's question. Maggie didn't know what was happening to her.

"Your mother, I presume?"

"Yes."

Jordon sat on the step beside Maggie. "That didn't sound like a happy conversation."

"No."

"Do you want to talk about it?" He wrapped an arm around her waist and pulled her to his shoulder.

"Crystal is getting married. Although I'm not sure how that's even legal, since Paul is already married." Maggie felt like crying, but she refused the relief. With a deep breath, she reminded herself that, like all emotion, the worry and sorrow would pass.

Jordon rubbed her arm. "We can't pick our parents, and we can't make their decisions. They're adults. They screw up on their own."

He spoke the truth, so why was she opposed to the notion?

Pushing him away, Maggie stared into his clear eyes. The reflection of her frazzled face in the glossy pools of black startled her. So many wrinkles and contortions lined her face. And yet when she looked at him, he was smooth and serene. The role reversal didn't seem fair.

"Maybe that applies to your father, but not to my mother. She's different. She's weakened by a too-big heart and a naïve mind, and this chauvinist is taking terrible advantage of her." Maggie dropped her face to her hands and rested her elbows on her knees. The hurtful words flying off her lips left her with a terrible taste in her mouth. Still, she couldn't seem to calm her fears.

"I think you're taking on too much responsibility where your family is concerned." Jordon slipped a hand over the bend in her back.

"Maybe you're not taking on enough." She spoke into her hands, hoping he didn't hear, but his hand dropped off her back, and she knew the words managed to leak out.

"What's that supposed to mean?" His black brows pulled together atop his flaring nose, and his teeth tore into the flesh of his bottom lip.

"Jordon, you should mend relations with your family. That sort of karmic implication is devastating."

He didn't lighten, and when he spoke he sneered. "And you know this how? Because Buddha told you?"

He was patronizing her, and she deserved it. Her attack on his relationships amounted to nothing more than projection, a pitiful attempt to distract him from analyzing her feelings about Crystal. "It's what I believe."

"Well, it's not what I believe." He stood, towering over her as she stared at the empty field and listened to his heavy breathing.

Maybe she hoped to do more than distract him. Maybe her meddling meant to push him away. An angry Jordon was far less likely to love her. And if he didn't love her, she could go back to living life without the onslaught of heady emotions.

She rolled her head slowly until she saw his gloomy face. "Jordon, what *do* you believe?"

He shoved his hands in his jean pockets and stared off into the distance. "I don't know."

"That's what I thought. If you don't know what you believe, how can you demean what I believe?"

Their eyes locked. "Just because I'm not sure what I believe doesn't mean I don't have some thoughts, and the idea that karma determines my outcome doesn't seem right."

"Why not?"

"Maggie, look at it from my perspective. I was a good kid. I did what everyone expected me to do, and I still ended up with a dead mom and a loser dad who stole my money. On the other hand, I've been a pretty lousy man. I've lied, bullied, belittled, and taken advantage of weaker people, but the universe, your universe, keeps rewarding me. I have more money, more houses, more cars and now you. Explain how that's possible if karma exists?" He squatted next to her and grabbed her hand.

She blinked back tears. "Jordon, karma isn't instantaneous. What you're doing in this life impacts your next life, and on and on and on. Your money, your success, that's all a gift because somewhere along the line in past lives you were generous enough to earn them. The negative stuff works the same way. You caused it by your behavior in a past life, and your current negative behaviors are going to haunt you in future lives. That's karma. That's how it works." She was breathless from the speed of her speech.

He stared right through her. "You don't know that any more than Carlos knows the Blessed Virgin awaits him in heaven. It's all mystical mumblings to make the guilty feel forgiven and the scared feel better about dying. What if there's nothing, Maggie? What if when you close your eyes there's no heaven, no second life, just darkness?"

She wilted, wrapping her arms around her stomach and leaning forward to drag in a miserable breath. She stared at the dirty concrete beneath her feet. Silent seconds passed with her trying to form a rebuttal. And then there it was, amid the filth on the ground, crystals shimmering in the filthy cement.

Drawing air deep into her belly, Maggie softened her muscles before looking at Jordon. "I could never believe in nothing." She rubbed her hand over his pulsing cheek, stroking his smooth skin until his jaw relaxed. "I've seen both dark and light exist simultaneously. I don't believe a place can ever be void of either. Where there is dark, there is light. Even in your scenario, there is still light—somewhere. There has to be. The light is what people call heaven. No matter how dark, the question always is...where is the light?"

*

Jordon was staring at it. Bright and blinding. Maggie's eyes were wide with unshed tears and unconditional love. He wanted to drop to his knees and confess every sin he'd ever thought to commit—such an absurd reaction for a man like him. All these years, he confessed nothing. He acted, reacted and reaped the benefits. He also bore the scars.

He wasn't ready to call his father, but maybe Grey. Maybe he could contact the kid without the old man being involved.

"Jordon?"

He blinked to focus.

"Are you okay?"

Better than okay. Something was happening inside of him, and he couldn't think to call it anything other than a thaw. He pulled her into his arms, and he knew without a doubt...he loved her.

Jordon held onto the words, preferring to save them for another time, a time when she would believe him. "I'm fine, and I'm sorry if anything I said upset you."

With her head against his chest, her body relaxed. "I'm sorry, too. You're right. Crystal is an adult, and I should stop making decisions for her."

"That's easier said than done," Jordon said, tightening his grip.

Maggie nodded against him. "It's just that I've spent my whole life worrying about her. I bet I've spent every past life worrying about her too."

All the talk about karma and death and multiple lives replayed in Jordon's head. Maybe Maggie was right. Maybe he needed to pay closer attention to his actions and how they would impact him and the people he loved long after he'd gone. "Maggie?"

She looked at him from her restful spot, snug in the crook of his arm.

"If we have more than one life, does that mean we've met before, and will we be together again?"

Something in her watery eyes told him yes, but then she buried her face in his chest. "I don't know."

He dropped his nose to the top of her head and pressed his lips to her velvet hair, breathing in a scent so strong and familiar that sparks of light filled him. The ensuing peace was enough confirmation for him. "Well, that's what I believe. And you know what else I believe?"

She looked at him again. "What?"

"If we don't get to the grocery store soon, that turkey in the refrigerator will be mighty lonely on Thanksgiving Day."

*

Maggie and Jordon shopped while Carlos worked with team trainers. Maggie pushed a cart mounded with what Jordon said was enough supplies to feed seven people Thanksgiving dinner. By her estimate, there was enough food to feed an entire baseball team.

"You're going to cook all this by yourself?" She eyed him suspiciously.

"No. You're going to help me."

She looked over his right shoulder to a freezer case filled with headless turkeys like the one tormenting her in the refrigerator. "Maybe Bernie should help instead."

Jordon laughed and tossed a pound of unsalted butter onto the heap. "If Bernie helps, you'll get gizzards in your stuffing."

She wrinkled her nose. "Fine. Just don't ask me to touch the poor bird."

"Hey, that bird has blissfully embarked on his next life by now."

Jordon's adoption of her philosophies only deepened her worry that transference was the reason for his attraction to her.

The edges of his eyes crinkled as his lips curved into a smile. He was joyful, while she battled her beliefs and common sense. The transformation he'd undergone made it all the more difficult to tell him she couldn't risk getting closer to him. The sex had been a mistake. She couldn't keep leading him on and confusing herself.

The grocery store was not the place for that discussion.

"Are you making fun of me?" she asked, deciding to keep the conversation light.

Jordon stopped before she had time to react, and the cart slammed into his left hip.

His eyes narrowed. "Ouch. I wasn't making fun of you. If I were making fun of you, I would say something lame about women drivers, since you rear-ended me." He smiled and reached into the cooler for a package of cream cheese. "I'm serious about the bird. I rather like that scenario."

"Because I like that scenario?" She held her breath, waiting for his answer.

"Sure. And I'm going to call Grey."

She wanted him to reconcile with his family—but not to please her. "Why are you calling him?"

"Why not? I thought that's what you wanted?"

Maggie swiveled her head a few times until an elderly lady passed and left them in relative private. "I want you to contact your family for you, not to prove something to me."

Jordon crossed his arms over his chest in the defensive manner she'd grown accustomed to. "Maggie, do you really want to have this conversation here?"

"No, I don't, but...we have to have it somewhere."

"How about in the bread aisle? I need rolls." He walked away.

"Jordon, I'm serious."

She startled when he spun around and grabbed the end of the cart with both hands before she could plow into him again. "No you're not. If you were serious, you would stop treating me like a flaky patient. I thought we made progress at the stadium, but I was wrong. You don't think I know what you're doing, how you're looking at me? There's enough pity in your eyes to drown a third world country."

People were staring now. "Jordon, I changed my mind. Let's not do this here. It's not an appropriate place."

His angry eyes flashed at the few people who shared the toothpaste aisle with them, but their presence did nothing to deter him. "You started it, and I'm going to finish it."

"Fine." She let go of the cart, her arms landing across her chest. "You can't fall in love with me."

The nearest couple hastened down the aisle amid whispers. A lone woman remained, studying a tube of Crest with one ear peeled to the drama.

Jordon nodded tightly, his arms still wrapped around his body. "Is that so?"

"Yes, it is. What you're experiencing is called transference, and you're transferring your affectionate feelings to me because you're repeating a pattern of emotion from your childhood. It's Freudian and I'm to blame, because I created a nurturing environment where I've given you help with Carlos and..." Maggie's gaze flitted to the woman studying the same tube. "...the other thing."

Jordon followed the direction of her eyes, turning his head and spying the interloper. He angled back at Maggie, and his lips stretched over his white teeth. His smile made Maggie wish she'd kept her big mouth shut, but by the look of the mischievous sparkle in his eyes, she was too late.

"The other thing? You mean the sex. I'm transferring feelings of love to you from my childhood because we have hot, sweaty sex. The best sex I've ever had."

The woman dropped the tube, and Jordon walked toward her. "Let me get that for you, ma'am." He bent down, and handed the toothpaste to the gaping woman, who wandered aimlessly down the aisle until she disappeared, forgetting her cart.

"That was uncalled for." Maggie shook her head and bit back a laugh.

Jordon didn't stop at the end of the cart. He came around and grabbed her by the hips. "We're done with this conversation. I'm not going to let you push me away because of your misguided notions and over-analysis."

She opened her mouth at his absurd insults, but before she could say a word, his fingers rested on her chin and closed her jaw.

"Maggie, transference is bullshit. Freud was a flake. You shrinks like to wield power over weak-minded patients. I'm not weak, and

I'm not your patient." He slid his thumb across her bottom lip. "I do...feel exactly the way I said I do, but I won't say the words until I'm damn sure you're going to say them back. Until then, keep your shrink wrap away from my head. There's enough going on in there without you digging around."

Despite the hypnotic sensation of his thumb stroking her lip, she couldn't keep quiet anymore. "I find you offensive."

"No, you don't."

He leaned his face closer, and she swallowed. Her tongue reflexively brushed over her lip, tasting the tip of his thumb. He stepped into her, and she swallowed again, knowing his mouth would be covering hers in the middle of a busy supermarket. But the minute his arm wound around her waist, she didn't care where they were. She wanted him to take what he wanted and leave her begging for more.

Jordon stopped inches from her mouth, his smiling eyes locked with hers. "Not here. This is not an appropriate place."

Her jaw dropped again. "That's what *I* said."

He lifted his head and set his broad shoulders. "Bread aisle. I need rolls."

Maggie gripped the cart with shaking hands. "You need a lobotomy. Something is not right with you." Her heart was racing. She didn't know whether to push the cart away as fast as she could or grab a handful of dental floss and pitch it at his gorgeous, gloating face.

"What?" He feigned innocence. His eyes wide, his brows high on his head. He even had the audacity to shrug. "What did I do?"

Trying to steady her breath, Maggie clamped her teeth together before she spoke. "Your negotiation tactics are suspect."

He winked. "Never. Now move your cute little ass to the bread aisle before I change my mind and make you beg."

Maggie huffed and pushed the cart by him. Her face felt fifty shades of inferno, and her hands were still shaking. As she rounded the corner, she came face to face with the woman holding a tube of Crest.

The woman took one look at Maggie and stammered. "That's my cart."

Maggie glanced at the contents and realized the woman was right. "Oh. I'm sorry." She stepped back and bumped directly into the reason for her scattered, damned soul.

"This is our cart, love."

Jordon's silky voice and the outlandish moniker goaded her on purpose, but Maggie was entirely too shaken and—dare she say it—turned on to think of a decent rebuttal.

The woman smiled. "You two are better than anything that's on cable. Good luck." She nodded, waved and waddled away with her cart in her hands.

"That was nice." Jordon squeezed Maggie's shoulders.

"That was insane."

"Then it's a good thing you have lots of experience in that department. I have a feeling sanity—or lack of it—is going to be a common theme in this relationship."

He had no idea. But Maggie did. This conversation wasn't over. She fully intended to have the last word…at home.

CHAPTER THIRTEEN

"What do you mean you can't sleep with me again?" Jordon poked the sharpened tip of the paring knife into the cutting board and glared at his angel of frustration.

Maggie sat on a stool at the kitchen island, chopping Granny Smith apples into precise one-inch squares. They'd been talking about how a lake house with a pier needed a boat. There was nothing controversial until her last random statement. And now that she said it, she refused to look at him, even when his knife hit the board and stuck straight in the air.

"Jordon, you don't scare me." She kept cutting.

"Damn it, Maggie, yes I do. If I didn't scare you, you would look at me."

She did, and she couldn't hold the intensity of his gaze for more than two seconds before she stared at the apples again. "I can't look at you and cut. I'll hurt myself."

He reached over and grabbed the wrist connected to her cutting hand. "Then stop and explain yourself."

She dropped the knife, and her oversized eyes settled on his face. "If I sleep with you again, I'm only perpetuating the idea that we have a future together, and we don't. That's impossible." She looked serious. Her lips didn't twitch. "Attachment is dangerous, and romantic love is a lie disseminated by greeting card companies and Hollywood movies. Love is a word we use to describe an obsessive need to possess. The possession leads to loss, and the loss leads to pain. I don't want to cause either one of us pain." She turned her palm over to hold his hand in hers. "Okay?"

They were the stupidest words he'd ever heard. He jerked his hand away and walked to the corner of the counters, wedging himself into the ninety-degree angle, gripping the cold marble in his hands.

"No. It's not okay. You don't make any sense. Do you even believe what you're saying or do you just spit out words that have been force-fed to you by your mother?" He clenched his teeth, and a growl escaped. "You're the craziest woman on the planet." He wanted to shake the serenity off her beautiful face. "And the apples need to be in thin slices, not squares."

Maggie looked down at the pile in front of her and then back to him. "Why didn't you say something before?"

"Because I didn't want to hurt your feelings." Although, he imaged the bite in his voice would take care of that.

"Are you mad because I cut them wrong?"

"No." He growled again. "You just casually informed me we can't have sex because we don't have a future together. I'm mad because you're done with me." He snapped his fingers. "Just like that."

"Not just like that. I've been thinking about it for a while."

"Oh, great. So while I'm thinking we're amazing together and you're bound to realize we're meant to be, you're thinking of ways to stop being with me. Whatever, Maggie. I'm done trying to figure you out." He grabbed a dish towel and threw it into the sink, sealing his tantrum. "Go. Lock yourself in your room and figure yourself out. After I finish this pie, I'm going to bed, and unless you're willing to get naked, stay the hell out of my room."

He sounded a lot meaner than he felt. He was upset all right, but he didn't want to go to bed alone. He enjoyed the sparring. In some ways, it was the best foreplay he'd ever had. Unfortunately, he doubted it was headed in that direction tonight. Maybe tomorrow, after they'd both had a good night's sleep.

Only, Jordon didn't sleep. He tossed and turned, somehow still managing to roll out of bed before the sun—like every other day. Burning daylight meant deals went undone and opportunities missed. Even holidays had obligations.

Shoving the covered turkey into the oven, he walked to the

sink. With his hands busy under the hot water, he didn't bother covering his mouth when he yawned. Instead, he shook his head until the sleepy gasp passed. He'd always been a night owl and an early bird. He wasn't sure there was a cliché to describe him, so he settled on one word: insomniac. He didn't believe the sleeplessness could get any worse until last night.

He loved Maggie. Months ago, she walked into his life without knowing the conflict she'd caused him, and last night, despite the conflict, he determined to never let her go. Around three A.M., he went to her, to tell her that despite the endless array of things she said and did that left him bewildered, he felt whole and satisfied for the first time in his empty life. But when he met with a locked door, he figured she was in no mood to listen.

He stomped a pedal, lifting the lid on the trash can and tossing a wadded paper towel inside. Yawning again, he balked at the chores in front of him but ultimately refused to give up. A promise was a promise, and he promised Maggie the best Thanksgiving. In his mind, the best Thanksgiving started with cooking a gourmet meal together and ended with a vigorous roll in the sheets. He would have to improvise.

Before Jordon got lost in food prep, his phone rang, sinking his heart. Early morning calls were never a good sign, especially on a holiday. During the season, he would suspect anything from torn ACLs and ulnar collateral ligaments to concussions. During the off-season, DUIs and sexual assault allegations topped the worry list.

He blinked, unable to believe the name flashing across his BlackBerry's screen. "Hello?"

"I got your message."

Jordon left the message last night after a glass of whiskey and a couple rounds of solitaire. He didn't expect his brother to return the call. "Grey...I'm happy you called."

"You're surprised I called."

"That too."

"Thanks for leaving that message. I, uh, know it couldn't have been easy." A loud sigh echoed on the line. "Happy Thanksgiving, J."

Grey sounded older and more tired than Jordon remembered. "Happy Thanksgiving to you, too, man."

There was more to say, complicated explanations and apologies Jordon had perfected in his head over the years, but now that the time had come to say those things, he didn't want to risk souring the conversation. "So what's been going on?" he asked, preferring to keep his brother on the phone.

"Not much. Been playing a lot of X-Box. I don't know what to do with my hands in the off season."

"I bet. You had a good season. Seventy stolen bases."

"Yep."

"You always were the faster one." And just like that, darkness crept in. Jordon remembered Grey ducking out of the old man's way before another fist landed against the boy's tanned skin. Grey got away. Jordon didn't. "How's the old man?" he forced out through clenched teeth.

Cavernous silence made Jordon think he'd lost Grey before they even had a chance to start over again.

But then came a noisy breath followed by slow words. "I don't know. He bought a place in Bermuda last year. I haven't talked to him since. You know how it goes."

Jordon wasn't sure if that was an invitation to ask for more details or to rehash the particulars about Grey's draft, but he didn't dare take it further, not if he wanted his brother back in his life. "Yeah, I know. Are you hanging with Lindsay's family today?"

Although Jordon had only met her once, he'd heard through mutual friends that Grey was still with his high school sweetheart. "No. She…uh…she moved to Bermuda with him."

Jordon's BlackBerry clattered to the countertop amid a barrage of vulgarities. He snatched the phone, inspected it quickly and pressed it to his ear. "I want you on the next plane to Charlotte."

"I'm fine."

"The hell you are. You either get on a plane, or I'm coming to you."

After a few more minutes, Grey agreed to catch a flight and Jordon added an extra plate to the pile in front of him. When he hung up, he counted the chairs around his dining table.

Something told him he'd remember this day. The question was, would those memories be good or bad?

*

Even though the turkey's head was missing, Maggie had a hard time believing the bird on the table wasn't staring at her. She tried to take her mind off the cooked carcass by studying the pandemonium around her.

Bernie's daughters fought over a pink bendy straw while Tabitha's eyes bugged out of her head. She gripped both girls around the wrists and hissed. Bernie reached over them all, plucking the pink straw from the little one's glass. He marched to the trash can and ceremoniously disposed of the offensive culprit amid loud whines of protest.

On the other side of the table, Carlos smoothed a white linen napkin over his lap and talked baseball with Jordon and his brother. With the exception of a couple inches in height and width, Grey looked identical to Jordon.

Sitting at the long table opposite Jordon, Maggie felt privileged and foolish. After the way she behaved last night, she had no right to be at the head of his table, like his queen. She tried to put Bernie in her place, even offered her seat to Carlos, but each time, Jordon stepped in to remedy the mistakes in his seating arrangements.

She watched him from across the table. He tipped his head back and laughed, and her heart pinched with jealousy. She berated herself for the errant emotion. Grey deserved Jordon's attention. After all, she didn't seem to want it. She pushed Jordon away. Hopefully, Grey wouldn't do the same.

Jordon raised a glass of red wine above his head and cleared his throat. "I thought about starting with a Thanksgiving toast." He glanced at Maggie, and her stomach flipped. "But, instead, I think we should start with a prayer. Maggie, would you do the honors?"

She nodded and then dropped her head as silence fell over the house. Her swallow echoed in her ears. "Around this table are humble hearts eager for nourishment. We're thankful for the bounty before us..." she looked at the turkey "...especially the bird who gave life that we may eat."

The rest of the table's occupants glanced at her. A few chuckled. Maggie smiled. So did Jordon. Her heart squeezed.

She dropped her head again. "We're also thankful for the way you've touched our souls in the past days, weeks, months, years, and lives. We ask that you continue to bless us, guide us, and keep us in your care. Today and always. Amen."

A chorus of 'amens' rounded the table as Jordon lifted his glass. "Well done, Maggie." His eyes sparkled. "Now, a toast to family. You are all my family. Grey is my flesh and blood, and his presence at this table means more than words. That being said, the rest of you are just as much a part of me. I'm thankful for all of you. Cheers."

Maggie raised her water goblet to her lips and watched Jordon drink deeply from his wine glass. The squeezing in her chest intensified, and the craziest thought popped into her head...she wanted Jordon to love her—for real. She wanted to sit at the head of his table because she belonged there as his mate, his partner, his other half.

He passed a bowl of mashed potatoes to Grey and laughed again. All she could think about was how she wanted Jordon to laugh with her. She couldn't believe the clarity. It didn't matter that he was jaded and scarred, driven and serious, and too rational for his own good. It didn't matter that she was indecisive, imaginative, wishy-washy and wandering. All that mattered was somehow, while she was worrying about Jordon's mistaken love for her, she'd fallen terribly and torturously in love with him.

Her fork dropped, clanging against the plate and making the little ones scream.

"Sorry!" Maggie flattened her shaking hand over the utensil and tried to breath. The air felt heavy and hot. Her stomach churned and her head spun. "I…uh…I'm not feeling well."

She gripped the side of the table and pushed to stand.

Jordon stood. "What's wrong?"

"Nothing. I…" *Love you.* Her head said the words as her muscles went weak, her knees buckled and the world went black.

When Maggie opened her fuzzy eyes, she tried to focus on Jordon's voice.

"This is becoming a habit," he said.

She reached toward the pain on her forehead, barely touching the spot before the sting split her head in two. "Ouch."

"And this time, nobody was talking about polygamy."

He held a cold rag to the wounded skin and smiled. His warm breath brushed across her face and she recognized the smell of butter. The scent made her stomach rumble, reminding her of exactly where she'd been before she took her nose dive. She tried to lift her head off the pillow, and the pain skyrocketed.

The soft mattress cradled her body. "How did I get here?"

"I carried you."

Great. She was the circus freak of the Thanksgiving feast. "How long have I been out?"

"It's only been about five minutes of semi-consciousness. I was getting ready to drive you to the ER. Still might." He peeled back the cloth on her head and leaned in for a closer look.

Maggie closed her eyes to cope with more than the pain in her head. Snippets of her revelation slipped through the throbbing in her heart.

"It was the turkey, wasn't it? I figured you were putting on a brave face." He chuckled. "You were staring at me like you…I don't know. You were staring at me with this odd look, and then you dropped like dead weight. Was it the turkey leg in my hand?"

How could she blame the innocent bird for her behavior? Then again, how could she not? The carcass offered her a way out. If she blamed the bird, Jordon wouldn't ask more questions, questions she wasn't sure she was ready to answer. "I like turkeys."

"So do I."

"But I prefer mine alive."

He laughed again, and she tried to smile. The muscle movement in her forehead hurt too much.

"Take these."

Maggie opened her palm and Jordon dumped three red pills into her hand. He shoved an arm underneath her back and pulled her to semi-sitting, and then he reached for a glass of water with his free hand. Cradling her in his arms, he brought the water to her lips and poured a couple drops into her mouth.

She loved him, but she couldn't relax, couldn't be thankful. Falling in love didn't solve anything. It just begged more questions. If she loved him, wasn't it possible he loved her? And not because of transference? Maggie squeezed her eyes shut, trying to imagine such a thing through the pain and confusion in her head, but she couldn't believe it, couldn't see how they'd fit. Dealing with all her drama would surely chase him away, and then she'd become the broken half. Maggie swallowed her convoluted thoughts, along with the lingering feeling of stuck pills.

"Go back to your guests," she finally said.

"No way. You fell hard. I won't leave you alone until I know you're okay."

Fell hard. An ironic choice of words.

A tap on the door brought Jordon to his feet and sent him across the room.

"Need anything, Boss Man? How's the patient?" Bernie asked, sticking his head around Jordon's shoulders to smile at Maggie.

"Hi, Bernie. I'm fine. Sorry to ruin dinner."

"You didn't ruin anything. Now, if you'd fallen in the mash potatoes, we may've had a problem."

She tried to smile amid the two men's laughter, but the sting halted her again.

"We're good, Bernie. I'm going to stay with her for a while before I decide if I'm taking her to the ER."

"No ER," Maggie said.

"Now, listen here. If Boss Man says you're going, you're going. You may be a doctor, but he's bigger and meaner."

Jordon shoved Bernie's chest. "I'll give you mean. Out. Go entertain my brother." He shut the door and returned to Maggie's side. "Not exactly the best Thanksgiving ever. I'm sorry. I wanted to give you something you'd never forget."

How could she ever forget the moment she realized romantic love wasn't some hokey societal experiment gone wrong? The pain in her heart trumped the pain in her head, and she closed her eyes. If she told him she loved him and wanted to be with him, he would pull her close and say the words right back. She was tempted—very tempted—but she couldn't stop the voice of doubt. She suspected one day he'd wake up and realize he wasn't in love with her at all, that he respected her and needed to work through deep feelings from a rocky childhood and failed marriage, and Maggie was the body he needed to get past the spiritual pain. Then Jordon would leave her, and she'd be broken.

"I'm taking you to the ER."

"No! Why? I'm fine." She opened her eyes and tried to lift again.

"You're not fine. You look miserable. Something isn't right."

"Jordon, I'm fine. I'll be fine. Just let the medicine kick in. Please." It would help her head but not her heart.

"Maggie, you frustrate me. Why won't you let me take care of you?" He rested his head on the pillow next to hers and gathered her into his arms.

He felt strong and safe, and he smelled heavenly. Maggie wanted to detach from everything but him.

Unfortunately, Jordon was the one thing Maggie missed for the rest of the evening. He took a call and never returned. Bolstered by the pain meds, she forced herself to the living room, where she smiled at Bernie's dancing girls and laughed at Carlos and Grey's reenactment of Abbott and Costello's *Who's on First.*

When the house fell quiet because everyone had either left or fallen asleep, Maggie only wanted to brood. Flipping to her other side, she looked at the bedside clock. For all she knew, Jordon remained glued to his BlackBerry. She saw him once when he poked his head into the kitchen, asking how she felt. Then he hurried off with his ringing phone in hand.

"There's been an accident," he'd called over his shoulder.

It must've been serious.

She thought about praying or meditating. Lately, she thought about doing those things a lot more than she ever did them. Running her fingernails over her upper arms, she tried to relax. After weeks of living with a non-stop parade of questions marching through her mind, only one remained: *Would it be so horrible to love someone who may or may not love me back?*

Maggie closed her eyes before she could settle on an answer. When she opened them, Jordon curled around her. She didn't know how long she'd been sleeping or when he appeared, but his breath blanketed her neck, convincing her he wasn't a dream. Warmth rushed through her, and she reached a hand to the strong arm wrapped around her stomach.

"Maggie, I'm sorry I missed the rest of the evening. Battaglia's been in an accident."

"Is he okay?"

"No. He's in surgery. I have to go help his family get things in order." Jordon pressed his nose into a soft spot on her shoulder, and he blew a shaky breath over her back. "He's in critical condition."

She squeezed his arm and turned to hold him. "I'm sorry."

"And I'm selfish. I'm torn between going and staying with you. Are you sure you're okay?"

"Jordon, go. They need you." She swallowed hard. "I..." The words were right there. She swallowed again. "I...need you, too, but I'm fine. They aren't."

He propped on an elbow to stare at her, and for a moment, Maggie thought she'd actually said the words she couldn't manage to say.

A slice of moonlight slipped through the wooden blinds and brightened his face. "What did you say?"

She fought against the impulse to close her eyes and shield her soul from his desperate gaze. "I need you, too." The whisper came from someplace deep inside of her. And although the words weren't precise, she suspected he caught her meaning.

Jordon shoved both arms underneath her and squeezed her against his chest. "Maggie, don't leave me. I don't know how long this will take. It could take until after Carlos goes. Please don't leave. Wait for me."

He brushed his lips against her throat, and she wondered how many times he begged his ex-wife to wait for him. He had so many unresolved issues. Maggie had unresolved issues, too, and yet... "I'll wait."

He propped on his elbow again and brushed his fingertips over the tender bump. "How's your head?"

She'd been so busy worrying about her feelings and consoling his, she'd forgotten about the injury. She frowned. "I could probably use more Advil."

He scrambled off the bed. "I'll be right back."

When he returned with the medication minutes later, he plumped her pillows, stroked her arms and stayed wrapped around her until he fell asleep with his BlackBerry propped on the headboard above him, his alarm set for 4 A.M.

She listened to him sleeping, but no matter how hard she tried, she couldn't find the same peace—she wouldn't until she revealed her feelings and dealt with the consequences

CHAPTER FOURTEEN

Carlos carried a basket filled with folded laundry on his hip. He stopped alongside the living room sofa and smiled at Maggie. "Do you have anything you want me to wash?"

She pushed out of Downward Facing Dog and dropped to her knees. "No, thanks, but I'm proud of you. You're going to make an excellent husband someday."

Sadness flickered across his face, and Maggie regretted the marital reference. She hadn't talked seriously with Carlos in days. With Jordon home, Carlos kept his distance, but now that Jordon was gone, the silence was going to change.

"Are you going home to tell your mother you're gay?" she asked.

Carlos looked surprised, like the thought had never crossed his troubled mind, but Maggie knew better. In her professional experience, the how and when of telling a parent became all-consuming.

Carlos wrinkled his nose. "I'm not telling her. Nobody's proud of a gay son."

"That's not true."

He rolled his eyes. "Name one."

She couldn't think of anybody, not because it didn't happen but because she didn't have the privilege of knowing anyone. "I know you're gay, and I'm proud of you."

"You're not my mother." He puckered his lips and cocked his head. "And Jordon…did you tell him?"

"I told you I wouldn't. He's happy enough with your progress on the mound that he hasn't asked about our conversations or how you got there."

"Good. Don't tell him. There's no gay in baseball. I play baseball," he said with a sharp nod.

Maggie felt miserable. She hated to see Carlos closing off. Enlightenment required openness to learning about the self and the world without judgment, without attachment and without fear. After more than a month of treading the waters in her own spiritual void, Maggie understood she might not be the best guide to enlightenment, but she was the only guide Carlos had.

"You can't hide your feelings," she said.

"I won't. Not forever. Just for now. When I retire, nobody will care what I do."

It was true. Was she wrong to feel relief? If Carlos believed what he said, then she'd done her job. She helped him come to terms with his sexuality and make a comfortable decision.

They both knew he couldn't be openly gay in baseball without suffering a tremendous amount of pressure and ridicule. A pitcher's greatest asset was his steadfast mind and unshakable confidence. She didn't see how Carlos could maintain his on-field performance with off-field stress. He'd be singled out and mentally tortured for being different. This was the easiest way—for everyone.

Maggie stared at the shirtless young man. "You'll still need to talk to someone. Hiding your feelings won't be easy. You're only twenty. That's a lot of years playing baseball without love and support from a partner."

He seemed to think about his lonely future. His forehead bunched, and the corners of his lips dropped. "I can talk to you."

"Yes, you can. But you need a support network bigger than one person."

That was always the hardest part for a client to understand. After the initial breakthrough, life seemed doable as long as Maggie was there to guide them, but that wasn't the goal. A good therapist wanted her clients to fly the proverbial nest, stronger and more capable, not remain dependent.

"What about your sisters? Can you talk to them?"

"No." He shifted the basket to his other hip and shuffled to the stairs.

While on the surface Carlos sparkled with a ninety-nine-mile-per-hour fastball and an engaged personality in Jordon's presence, he lacked plausible direction and risked another breakdown. Despite that, some psychologists would walk away, claiming success for Carlos's return to the mound. Maggie wasn't one of them.

"I think you should tell Jordon." She knew the suggestion was controversial.

Carlos turned and narrowed his eyes.

"Follow me on this, okay?" Not a muscle in his body flinched. He stood ready to fight, and Maggie felt unsure of her approach for the first time in years. "Jordon's your agent. You trust him with the smallest details of your life, and from what I see he's a father figure to you. So if you can't talk to your mother, talk to him."

Carlos scoffed and tackled the first three stairs before Maggie's voice stopped him. "If you're committing yourself to baseball, then what's the big deal if he knows you're gay? We can tell him together when you get back, and then he'll have a better understanding of who you are, and you'll have someone else's support." She hoped… but a part of her worried about Jordon's reaction.

Carlos hoisted the basket higher on his hip and disappeared.

Two days later, he was gone, and Maggie tried to fill her days. When she wasn't conducting virtual therapy sessions with her girls, she thought about Jordon, hoping everything was okay. By now she was used to his narrow focus when he was away from home. She didn't expect to hear from him, and somehow she'd come to accept it. Abbreviated telephone conversations did nothing but leave people longing for more words and face-to-face contact. Maybe that's why she made no attempts to call Crystal. Maggie couldn't imagine anything her mother saying putting her mind at ease.

When the temperature turned unseasonably cold, Maggie thought about asking Bernie for a ride to the shopping mall to buy a warmer coat. Then she could at least go for walks outside. But when it came down to it, she didn't want to interrupt his family and study time. So she stayed locked inside Jordon's house, and when the rain pounded against the skylights, she unrolled her yoga mat, unfurled her tense body and stared at the droplets rolling down the glass. Cultivating her inner silence felt better than spending another minute thinking about Carlos, worrying about Crystal and missing Jordon.

When she meditated on the sight of the rain drops long enough to feel her breathing slow, she switched to meditating on sound. She listened to the thump of droplets hitting the window glass, and then she reached beyond the house to the rustling leaves.

Maggie welcomed the increasing focus and clarity, until the warm calm gave way to a chill. She was alone with the house all to herself. Space as far as the eye could see.

Wasn't that what she wanted? Space? A house of her own?

The trip to North Carolina provided distance from Crystal, whose teachings no longer ran amuck in Maggie's head. That was a good thing, right? Now Maggie had silence and independence enough to make her own decisions about her future, a future that might or might not include Jordon. She expected to feel happy about that. Instead, she felt restless, unstable…exhausted.

Maggie curled in the overstuffed chair nearest the lake view. Crystal taught her to look inside for answers, but Maggie was tired of being alone with her thoughts. She wanted to talk to someone, to share with someone, to feel connected to someone, even if that connection would eventually break. She touched her hand to her pounding heart as chills engulfed her body. All the time she spent searching for detachment, a solitary peace, she should've spent making connections. Even Crystal ended up going against the teachings she held so dear.

Tears streamed down Maggie's cheeks. She chastised Jordon for not knowing what he believed, but she was no better. Her beliefs were convoluted and didn't stand up to the slightest test. What if everything she ever believed in was wrong? What if Jordon was right? What if in the end there was nothing?

Once again, she lamented being too old for a quarter-life crisis, but too young for the midlife variety. And yet as she sat there, staring through tears at darkness descending upon the lake, she knew existential crises didn't pay attention to age. Plain and simple, she'd fallen apart. Could she put herself back together again?

Gripping her throat, Maggie milked the skin of her neck to aid a swallow. Breath became harder. Noises threatened from outside the house. She curled her knees to her chest, sliding down and deeper into the cushion of the chair.

Save me.

The saddest part was, she didn't know who she was praying to anymore.

When Maggie woke, Jordon was leaning over her, stroking the skin on her cheek. "Hey."

She blinked, yawned and reached for him without a word. He lifted her enough to settle his own body on the chair and cradle her in his arms.

She was his. He claimed her that night on the pier, and tonight she admitted it freely. Without him, the present lost its colors and the future loomed cold. Burying her head against his chest, she let a tear escape along with a quiet sob.

He lifted her chin. "What's wrong?"

She felt foolish, childish. Days of cluttered emotions and jumbled words pushed against her lips until she released the first thought in her head. "I don't want to be alone anymore." She gasped between snivels.

"I'm here."

Such sweet, simple words of reassurance, but frustration built inside of her. Did he understand the magnitude of what she was trying to say? Did she?

Maggie sat up in frustration. "I'm a mess. Things I thought were true probably aren't true. Maybe it's a nervous breakdown. At the very least, it's a personal crisis, and…" his bunched facial muscles reminded her she was expecting too much from a man who couldn't possibly understand her, "…I should go."

"What? Why?"

"Who wants to be around an unstable flake who cries herself to sleep, pondering the deeper mysteries of the universe? I don't even want to be around her, and I'm her."

Jordon cradled her throat, smoothing his thumb along her tightened jaw. A touch of humor curved his lips, but then the darkness in his eyes stole the smile. He looked away, over her head and out to the flashes of light bouncing off the lake.

Anger at her selfish behavior, overshadowed her frustration. "I'm so sorry. How is he?"

"Paralyzed from the neck down."

The lump in her throat thickened. While she was rambling on about her whacky inner-turmoil, Jordon had his own worries. "Maybe the doctors are wrong," she said, lacing the words with hope.

He slipped his hands to the back of her neck and rubbed his thumb over the bumps of her spine. "They're the best doctors in the business." Sadness clouded his eyes. "He'll never play ball again, but that's not the worst part. He got married last fall, and they wanted to start a family."

Maggie withered at the amount of hurt pooling in Jordon's eyes. Resting her head on his chest, she wrapped her arms around him, hoping that by holding him close she could assume some of his grief. The gesture made him shudder.

"He'll never feel his wife's arms around him again. Never be able to touch her…like this."

He smoothed a hand over Maggie's back, sliding along the bend of her shoulder and the curve of her hip. She rode the waves of his chest with the scent of his cologne stirring her desire.

"I need you." He brushed his lips to her forehead, burning away the fog on her brain, leaving one thing clear. She was done pushing him away.

Arching her aching body against his chest, she raised her lips in search of his. Jordon's eyes locked with hers moments before their mouths met, and truth flashed behind the pain. He loved her, and she loved him. Maggie couldn't deny him any longer.

The kiss confirmed the love. Instead of guided by desperation, his mouth softened, and his tongue glided over her lips, as if lapping her up one lick at a time was the only thing that mattered.

She brushed his jaw, and his tongue made another slow, gentle sweep inside her mouth. He dropped a hand from her shoulder and flicked a thumb over her nipple, moaning into her mouth when she nibbled his bottom lip. A strong, steady passion built in her chest, and Maggie knew it could be like this forever.

He pulled away and stared into her eyes, his thumb circling her nipple. "I can't live without feeling you like this. I can't imagine it."

She stood and pulled him by the hand through the living room to the bedroom. Inside the door, he gripped the hem of her ruffled tunic and drew the cotton over her stomach, skimming past her breasts. With the fabric gripped between his fingers, he slid his palms over her arms until the shirt disappeared.

She reached for the buttons of his shirt.

"Not yet."

Sinking her teeth into her bottom lip, she willed herself to let go, to take without giving and to enjoy every minute. He smoothed his hands over her tingling skin, first her shoulders and arms and then her face. Her very essence demanded more, moving her body toward his touch until her head swayed in his hands.

Maggie fluttered her eyelids open, and in the soft glow of the bedroom she saw him watching her move with each stroke of his hand. He leaned in and kissed her, letting his hands drop lower until he cupped her breasts.

She'd never begged a man for anything, but standing before Jordon, her independence shattered. "Please."

"Please what?"

The hoarseness in his voice and the sleepy circles of his thumbs around her nipples made the need unbearable. "Love me."

Like their first kiss in the kitchen, he grabbed her and drove her backward until they both collapsed on the bed. She reached for his shirt buttons again, but he caught her wrists and shook his head a moment before his fingers dipped underneath the waistband of her pants.

Seconds stretched to minutes, and the minutes dragged on. Maggie sprawled across the bed without clothes, but she had the overwhelming feeling he wouldn't be happy until she was completely transparent. Jordon refused to cover her with his body, and each time she closed her eyes, he demanded that she open them. His hands possessed every curve until her greatest task was to breathe. And then he slid a hand between her legs.

Maggie reached for his neck, but he pulled away. "Jordon, this is unbearable."

"Then I'm doing it right."

No argument there. She closed her eyes and moved against his hand.

"Do you want me to stop?"

"No."

"Then open your eyes."

She tried. She sent the message to her brain, but the heat between her legs spilled into her gut and threatened to burn a hole in her heart.

"Maggie, look at me."

His voice was little more than a whisper, and her reflex to please him forced her eyes open. Despite the lusty haze and the dim lighting, preventing her from focusing on the details of his face, she watched him watching her as his fingers continued to slip rhythmically over the swollen flesh between her legs.

Earthy noises escaped her lips, and she brought a hand between her teeth to stop from crying out.

Jordon smiled as he played with her breasts. "You're beautiful."

She managed words mixed with breathless laughter. "And you're merciless."

He slipped a finger deep inside of her, and she gasped.

"What's wrong?"

She closed her eyes again and quickened the rocking of her hips. "Nothing."

"Maggie."

She loved the way he said her name.

"Maggie."

It started pressed between his sweet lips, and rolled off his tongue like music.

"Maggie, open your eyes."

If he stopped now, she would die. Forcing her eyes open, she gripped the comforter in her hands and arched her back until her body trembled with the first waves of orgasm. "Jordon..."

The words were right there, dripping from her bottom lip and yet the room fell silent. Maybe she was too spent to speak a full sentence. "Jordon, I..."

"I know." He lifted over her and pressed his lips to hers, his hand tracing the curves of her breasts. "I know what you want to say." He brushed the bend of her shoulder with his lips. "That's why I wanted your eyes open. The windows to the soul."

She closed her hand over his, holding them both over her heart. Staring deep into the eyes she once found cold and lifeless, she saw the only future she ever wanted.

Desire stirred again as he rolled her aching nipples between his fingers and traced the curve of her chin with the tip of his tongue. "Jordon?"

"Yes?" His warm breath rushed across her ear lobe.

"Make love to me."

CHAPTER FIFTEEN

Jordon sat on the edge of the bed and thought about how far they'd come. He loved Maggie. Maggie loved him, and there was no bigger turn-on. The proof pressed against the seam of his boxers, and he squeezed the air from his lungs, hoping to relieve some pressure.

When her warm skin smoothed against his bare back, threatening his resolve, he stood. "Lay down, Maggie."

Faint light from the living room lit her face enough to reveal uncertainty. He flicked the clasp on his gabardines and let them drop to the floor.

She slid along his satin comforter until she settled against a wall of down-filled pillows. "Like this?"

"Like that." He stared a little too long, hoping to emblazon the dusky image on his brain. She belonged in his bed from the moment he first saw her, and now that she was here, he'd never let her go.

Crawling across the mattress until he covered her body with his, Jordon feasted on her lips and tongue. Beneath him, Maggie was different. She hesitated before every touch, her fingertips grazing his chest like she expected to be burned. The innocence drove him wild.

Jordon scooped her into his arms, burying his face in her neck. Their bodies aligned, and without any conscious direction or barrier between them, he slid inside of her.

He wasn't sure he could move, wasn't sure he wanted to. He knew he should put on a condom before he continued. Instead, he opened his mouth and sucked gently on the soft skin beneath her ear.

She wrapped her arms around him first, and then her long legs followed. Still, he couldn't move, and the quiet hardened him further.

"Jordon, please."

Her voice snapped his trance and then her hips stirred. He thrust once, and she cried out.

For a moment, he wondered if all the blood rushing to his lower half would knock him unconscious. He pushed inside of her again.

"Yes, please. Yes."

Again. He thrust as she begged and her legs tightened around his hips. The pace quickened, and he lifted his head to see her face. Her eyes were closed, her teeth shredding her bottom lip.

He wasn't sure he could speak, but he tried. "Open."

She dropped her legs and widened underneath him. The loss of pressure made the thrusts deeper, wilder. He lifted on quaking arms. "Your eyes. Open your eyes."

And when she did, he came inside of her. He should've pulled out. He planned to, but he got carried away. Even so, there was no regret, no worry.

For the first time in his adult life, he knew what he needed: a family.

*

If sex could change a life and enlighten a soul, sex with Jordon was that kind of sex. Maggie dropped her heavy head against the pillows and stared at the stars through the skylights above his bed. He wrapped around her and breathed against her neck.

Of course she loved him, but it was unlike anything she'd ever felt before. It was joyous and frightful all at once, like submitting to her desires and accepting the gift of his body was thrilling and scary, too. Light and dark—always combined—making the universe complete.

Just like Jordon completed her.

"Thank you." Those were the right words to say, weren't they? She didn't know. She'd never felt compelled to thank a man after sex. Then again, what happened between her and Jordon was so much more.

There was a big difference between having sex and making love. Jordon lifted his head. "Do you love me, Maggie?"

He knew she did. He said so moments before he rocked her with a physical connection that went beyond the world, but he deserved to hear her say the words.

"And not because I'm one of God's creatures." He attempted a smile. "Do you love me the way a woman loves a man? Do you love me because when you look at me you see all the answers to every question you've ever asked about yourself, about this life, and about what comes next?"

They were such beautiful words, shared on a perfect moment, their bodies still joined. She wanted to laugh and cry. "Yes. I love you like that."

He squeezed her. "Good, because that's the way I love you."

Maggie kissed the top of his head and rubbed her palms against the warm muscles of his back. Now what? She had a life outside these four walls, a fledgling career and a mother to worry about. He had another life, too; a demanding schedule keeping him awake all night and sending him to random destinations on a moment's notice. This would hardly be a traditional relationship. Then again, Maggie was hardly a traditional girl. She could return to Utah and visit him when their schedules permitted. He could visit her, too. A man like Jordon would welcome a relationship with no traditional strings attached.

He lifted his face from the bend of her neck. "What would you say if I asked you to marry me and have my baby?"

So much for no strings.

Before Maggie could answer, she was saved by the BlackBerry. An hour later, she remained naked in his bed, swinging between joyous acquiescence and nagging realism. This was life with Jordon Kemmons. One minute she melted in his strong arms, the next she doubted he even existed. If it weren't for the exotic location and the low hum of his voice in the other room, she might attempt to convince herself she was dreaming.

She could get up, get dressed and do something productive, but his final words paralyzed her. *Marry me. Have my baby.*

Sometimes Maggie already felt like a mother, what with Crystal's randomness and clients leaning on her for mental and emotional support. But would she know how to mother a real child?

She liked kids, liked the way they said what popped into their heads and did what their egos dictated. Kids lived pure and loved pure. They also required a lot of guidance, maybe more than Maggie could give. Doling out advice to people she kept at arm's length was different than guiding her own flesh and blood. It all came down to attachment.

Maggie slinked down the pillows and pulled the sheets higher over her breasts. Loving Jordon was a slippery slope. Falling for him amounted to the single greatest attachment. Having his children would simply add more. Could she live with that? Would she feel trapped? What if Maggie turned out to be like her mother, pushing everyone away in the name of detachment?

Jordon's shadow appeared before his body stood in the doorway. He leaned his shoulder against the doorjamb, and the light from the living room shone through the loose legs of his boxers.

"So this is what it's like to love a super hero?" She added a dreamy sigh for effect.

He set the BlackBerry on the dresser next to the door and crossed his arms over his broad chest. "I'm no super hero."

"That family would disagree." Maggie heard enough of the conversation as he walked from the room to know Buttaglia's father had been on the other end of the line.

Pulling the covers down on the left side of the bed, Maggie patted her hand on the mattress. "Come here, Spider Man."

His shoulders shook as he chuckled, moving toward her. "I thought you were scared of spiders." He gathered her into his arms.

"Not anymore." She weaved her fingers through the short, soft hairs peppering his pecs. "But I am scared of babies."

He smiled. "I expected marriage to scare you more than a helpless little baby."

"That's what scares me. What if I screw up?"

"You won't screw up."

"What if I'm like my mother?"

He kissed the top of her head and rested his chin where his lips had been, smoothing his hand over her upper arm as they lay in silence.

"What if I'm like my father?"

Belief forced her to her knees. "That's not possible. Jordon, you're going to be an amazing father! You take care of everyone."

He wound his arms around her waist and pulled her against his chest. "And you're going to be an amazing mother for the same reason."

She pressed her lips to his and opened her mouth so he could deepen the kiss.

He stopped abruptly, leaving her stomach filled with mushy lust. In the moonlight, his bold brow rose and his lips curled. "So it's a yes?"

"It's a maybe. I know that's not the traditional romantic answer, but I need time to work through the non-traditional parts of me."

He frowned.

"I love you." She knew the words would make him smile, even as they made her stomach flip. "I do. One thing at a time, okay? Marriage and a baby are sudden and unexpected ideas, and I have other obligations to consider."

"Like?"

"Like my career. If I agree to marry you and have your babies, then what?" He slipped a hand to her breast. One brush of his palm, and she melted. "Are you trying to distract me?"

"No. I'm trying to answer your question."

She nipped at his bottom lip. "Seriously?"

"Seriously."

"Where would we live?"

"Take your pick. I can live anywhere with an airport—and a bed." He nibbled her ear.

"It's not that easy."

"Sure it is. Do you like Salt Lake?"

"I do, but now that Crystal is gone, there's nothing keeping me there."

"So…if you could live anyway, where would it be?"

She looked around the darkened room, recalling the first time she entered. Her daydreams of climbing into this bed had turned into premonition. After all the resisting, here she was, and here she wanted to stay.

"I want to live here," she said, kissing him softly.

"Here in this bed or here in this house?"

Maggie smiled against his lips. "Both."

"Sounds good to me."

Jordon slipped his hand between her legs and wiggled his fingers dangerously close to her epicenter. As the flames climbed, Maggie decided further conversation could wait. Pulling her right thigh over his leg, her knee came to rest on the bulge in his boxers. She walked her fingers along his chest and planted soft kisses on the length of his neck.

Marrying this man seemed like a no-brainer. Not being with him amounted to torture. If having his baby was the only thing to worry about, Maggie should thank her lucky stars.

And she would as soon as…

The second phone call to interrupt them in as many hours kept Jordon away for only ten minutes, but when he returned to Maggie's side, his face was as twisted as it had been when he'd jumped out of bed to answer the phone.

"I have to go to New York."

The emotional roller coaster plummeted. "Now?"

"Tomorrow morning. It's a long story, but basically we suspect an employee of stealing from the corporation, and it's time for a confrontation."

He collapsed into bed with such force, Maggie's body lifted on a ripple of mattress. She smoothed a hand over his cheek to calm the pulsing in his jaw. He bore the worries of a father and the stress of a CEO. She felt his heart pound.

"Jordon, you can't..." Despite her worry, she couldn't finish the sentence. Telling him he couldn't do what he was born to do, be who he was meant to be, was not the way to keep him healthy and happy.

"I can't what?"

Maggie slid on top of him to straddle his hips. Running her palms from his chest to his shoulders, she pushed the heel of her hands into the knots. "You can't go until you're completely relaxed."

He gripped her waist. "Is that so?"

"Absolutely." She moved her fingertips in firm circles over the base of his neck. "I'm going to fix you before you get on that plane. And when you get home, I'm going to have to insist on a follow-up appointment. Right here. Like this." She dragged a palm to his throat and circled her fingers below his jaw.

He loosened on a moan. "Come with me."

Her rhythm slowed.

"Come to New York. We can shop for an engagement ring at Tiffany, and I can propose at the top of the Empire State Building."

She leaned forward and kissed him, which wasn't in her original plan for relaxation, but she didn't want to upset him with her words. "I can't."

When she rocked her pelvis, he gripped her bottom, and she knew desire was having a soothing effect.

He slipped his tongue over her earlobe. "Why can't you?"

"No proposal until I work through some things." She rocked against him until he was hard.

"For instance?" He slid a finger inside the folds of skin between her legs.

"My mother. She needs to know." *And Carlos. You need to know.* Maggie shuddered, unsure if the reaction was in response to Jordon's fingers moving inside of her, or the unpleasant thoughts marring her pleasure.

"So call her. Tell her. Now. Then we can fly to New York."

Tempting. So tempting. But... "I need to see her, talk to her face to face. Some things can't be settled over the phone." He nodded, and she knew he understood. "You go to New York. I'll go to Idaho, and we'll be back soon."

Then they could face the future together.

*

In what seemed like the blink of an eye, Maggie was in Idaho, staring at a river running through a picture-perfect landscape. The ribbon of water stretched until it dropped into the grayish horizon. She'd never seen anything more beautiful—except maybe Jordon's smile. She missed him, but coming here was the right thing.

"Magpie, breakfast!"

A tow-headed girl ran past and disappeared around the corner of the cedar shake farmhouse wearing nothing but a soft pink nightgown and a pair of too-big moonboots. Her name was Roselyn, and Maggie admired the gleam in her green eyes. More moxie lurked inside the five-year-old than most people collected in a lifetime.

Magpie. She'd been in Idaho long enough for the troops to refer to her with Crystal's pet name. Long enough for Maggie to realize she'd spent weeks behaving badly, judging people she didn't know and tuning out the people she did.

The trip turned out to be cathartic, and now she couldn't wait to get home to Jordon—and Carlos, where she would fix the final piece of the proposal puzzle and claim her own happy ending.

Maggie pushed her leather-covered toes into the flaky snow and shuffled toward the house. She smelled grilled potatoes wafting on the chilly wind and her stomach grumbled. She would be leaving Idaho soon, and with all the children under foot, she still hadn't found the right moment to tell Crystal she accepted her new lifestyle. She also hadn't talked about Jordon. After breakfast, when they washed dishes by hand and sang more than they talked, Maggie would try again.

She pushed the screen door open and offered a smile to the crew gathered around the rustic table.

"Fresh squeezed juice?" Crystal held out a hand-blown glass.

Crystal seemed more enamored with the workings of the herb farm and Paul's silver-haired father, Sander, than she did with Paul and Katherine, which helped Maggie relax.

"Magpie sits here." The little boy named Buck patted the end of a wooden bench.

A purple sprig of lavender rested on the white chipped plate in front of Maggie. Paul and Katherine's teenage daughter, Laurel, slid the flower behind Maggie's ear.

"It's flower communion today." Her voice was breathy and sweet. She looked pale and willowy like Paul, but with Katherine's mousy hair and complacent eyes.

"Thank you." Maggie wondered what it would feel like to see herself in the face of another living person. She looked at her mother and caught her own reflection in the dirty glass of a peeling hutch.

The rainbow of smells pulled her attention back to the table. Apples. Cinnamon. Toasted bread.

"Magpie, steel cut oats and almond milk?" Sander passed a fat bowl in Maggie's direction. He had hands like Paul's, long and pink, and while his eyes were the same opaque blue, the lines around them gave him an aged wisdom.

"Thank you."

Chatter lit the crowded room and mixed with the clangs of mismatched silverware on glass plates. They weren't traditional, but they were certainly family.

"How are you sleeping, Maggie?" Katherine smiled.

The high-pitched voice startled Maggie, even though she heard it often and without reservation on the farm. Katherine was nothing like Maggie imagined. Yes, she was submissive and open to alternative living arrangements, but she was also kind, intelligent, and selfless beyond the bounds of anything Maggie had ever witnessed.

Maggie had been wrong about her mother, too.

"How are you sleeping in the North bedroom, darling?"

"I'm sleeping well." Maggie stifled the urge to address Crystal as Mom.

Crystal smiled. "I know how you are about feng shui."

How I was. Maggie cast her gaze toward the bowlful of oats. Crystal expected the same Maggie. How could she not see the dramatic differences?

As if on a wave of telepathy, Crystal slid her chair from the table, stood and extended a hand to Maggie. "Come, love."

Protest built in Maggie's throat, but her lips pressed together and her hand slid into her mother's hand. Maggie expected a talisman, a lecture or incense burning to cleanse the troubled look of her soul. What she got was a story that changed her life.

When Crystal finally stopped talking, Maggie tried to process the information. "I imagined he died of an LSD overdose or still roamed the Himalayans as a sherpa," Maggie said, thinking back over decades of concocting grandiose stories to explain her missing father.

Crystal settled on the bed next to Maggie and pulled her hands into her lap. "Your father was a business man, and we met at the bank." A weak smile touched her wrinkled lips. "I was withdrawing my money from the hallmark of American greed, and he was depositing." Her chuckle tinged with sadness. "I told him he was exactly what was wrong with this great country, and he asked me to dinner."

"You went? With a stuffed suit?"

Crystal shrugged and her eyes turned dreamy. "He was... handsome. Tall, dark and powerful. He had the most ominous aura I'd ever seen, but something about him made it hard to say no."

Maggie gripped her mother's hands to steady the sway of irony threatening to toss her off the bed.

"I loved him, Magpie. I attached to him, threw myself at his feet and offered to give up everything to spend a single lifetime in his arms."

A horrible understanding grew beneath Maggie's rib cage and cut off air to her lungs. She recalled years of Crystal's preaching about the need for detachment. Maggie never realized the lectures came from experience. "What happened to him?"

Crystal cackled with despair. "He was married. He had a wife and kids on the other side of the country and came to San Francisco on business. I was the other woman, and I had no idea."

Crash. Crystal's words exploded in Maggie's ears. The ringing was unbearable. She stuffed her fingers against her drums and tried to block out her mother's pain.

Crystal smoothed a hand along Maggie's hips. "Magpie, you

need to hear this. I need to tell you. From the moment you arrived at the farm, I knew you couldn't leave without knowing the whole story. I should've told you long ago, but I wanted to protect us."

All those years. All those lessons. The spiteful words about romantic love. The distance Crystal cultivated with everyone she knew. Understandable results of an unbearable pain.

A tear slipped down Maggie's cheek, and she wished for Jordon to catch it.

"Darling, talk to me. Don't shut down. It's not good for you. Open."

"I love him." Maggie's chest heaved.

Crystal flinched. She didn't seem to understand Maggie's words. Her face scrunched and her head tipped to one side. "It's okay to love your father. He helped create you."

"No. I'm in love with Jordon Kemmons. I want to marry him." Maggie held her breath and braced for Crystal's reaction.

Crystal's face softened. "How wonderful. I'm so happy I didn't scar you for life." She pulled her into a hug. "Maybe we can have a double wedding right here on the farm. You, Jordon, me and Sander."

Maggie croaked on the emotion in her throat. "Sander?" And then she cackled. "Are you serious?"

Maggie's heart returned to the same steady beat, as she stared into a face she'd known for a lifetime, but didn't recognize.

Crystal laughed softly. "Yes, I am. If you'd given up on your prejudice against Paul and Katherine weeks ago, you wouldn't be so surprised." She kissed Maggie's nose. "I've been wrong about so many things, and I don't want you to struggle like I did. Being here with Sander helped me see that I was hiding from a pain that no longer existed. Time healed me, and if I hurt in the future, time will heal me again."

Maggie looked into her mother's warm eyes, deeper than she'd looked in a long time. "Where's my father now?"

"He died." Crystal's voice broke. "You were three months old. He was killed in a car accident on his way to the airport. That's how I found out about the wife. I expected to spread his ashes, but his body was returned to her."

Maggie imagined her beautiful mother with a baby on her hip and a gaping hole in her heart.

Crystal shrugged and squeezed Maggie's hand. "He's buried in Baltimore. I could find out the details if you want. You could visit."

"I don't want to."

"Not now, but maybe later. You have two half-brothers, Kyle and Clark. They look like you."

More stabbing. "How do you know?"

"They came to a coffee house concert a few years back. Their mother told them about me, and they thought it was cool that their father was associated with a famous singer." Crystal shrugged as if none of it were particularly important. "You should meet them. They're your flesh and blood, your family."

Loud laughter erupted from behind the closed door. Maggie imagined the Stratton kids playing tag around the kitchen table while Paul and Sander plucked on their guitars. Crystal smiled at the noises.

Maggie knew that look. It was the look of belonging, of wanting to be a part of something, of wanting to live and learn and laugh and grow with a group of people who knew you better than any other people on the planet. Connection. Family.

Kyle and Clark may be Maggie's flesh and blood, but they weren't her family.

She already had one of those.

CHAPTER SIXTEEN

Maggie unpacked her suitcase, returning her clothes to the drawers in Jordon's walk-in closet. She took a deep breath and drew in his smell, holding it in her lungs with her hands to her heart. She was home. She tried not to cry, but it wasn't easy. The monumental events of the last several days made her weepy.

When she'd finished unpacking, she adjusted the thermostat to seventy-two and pulled a sweater around her shoulders. She checked the clock every five minutes. Jordon's flight was delayed by bad weather in New York, and anxiousness stirred the hunger in her belly.

She made a bowl of rice and topped it with a handful of cherry tomatoes and slivered almonds. She missed the farm food. She missed Crystal. She even missed the rest of them. When she left for the long ride to the airport, they were gathered around a tree behind the house, hanging edible decorations from the boughs.

Taking in the neutral tones of the large walls around her, Maggie imagined a Christmas tree next to the fireplace and one on the deck strung with bird-friendly treats. A smile warmed her lips when she imagined the fit Jordon would pitch when her feathery friends dive-bombed his wood planks.

With the bowl in hand, she made her way around the kitchen island, passed between the dining table and hutch, and eased her exhausted body onto an oversized chair.

The front doorknob jiggled, and she whipped her head around to see two shadowy figures on the other side of the privacy glass. Her latest mouthful of rice caught in her throat, and she fought convulsive coughs rising from her chest. She stood, coughed some more and came face to face with Carlos and Bernie.

"You okay, Maggie?" Bernie rushed to her side, pounding her back a couple times.

She covered her mouth to stop her teeth from scattering on the floor. "I'm good." She stepped away from him before he could whack her again. "You guys scared me." She turned to Carlos who was already heading up the stairs. His face set in a blank stare and his knuckles whitened around a carryon bag. "You're home early."

He didn't speak as he disappeared.

She turned to face Bernie, letting an errant cough slip past her lips. "What's going on?"

"Who knows?" He shrugged. "I don't ask questions. I just give you people rides."

After Bernie left, Maggie knocked on Carlos's bedroom door. Talk about déjà vu. She wondered if this called for *House Hunters* and molding clay.

"Open, please. Let's talk. Why are you home early? Did you tell your family?"

Silence. She leaned against the door and knocked again. "I can help you, but I can only help if you help yourself. Come on, Carlos."

Nothing. She yawned and pressed a fist below her breast bone where a nagging burning sensation lingered from her Olympic-sized coughing fit. Forget it. She was bone tired.

"Don't worry about it, Carlos. I'm going to bed. We'll try again tomorrow."

She limped down the stairs and into the master bedroom where she undressed and crawled beneath the covers, taking care to use every last blanket folded at the bottom of the bed. Weeks of heavy emotion loosened their grip on her heart as she drifted off to sleep.

Maggie expected Jordon to rouse her with kisses, but instead she heard crying. Who was it? She stilled inside her darkened mind and listened. Was she dreaming?

When she felt a presence, her eyes shot open. A shadow loomed in the doorway. *Carlos.* His wails filled her with fear.

"What's wrong? What happened?" She wrapped an arm around the blankets and sat.

Moonlight sparkled on a stream of snot dripping from his nose. "What happened?" She was yelling, like Jordon.

"He...he...."

"He who?" She scrambled for a robe, not caring one bit if he glimpsed a bit of flesh in the process. "Did something happen to Jordon?" She raced toward Carlos, a heavy cramping in her gut.

"No. He's quitting."

"Who's quitting what?" Maggie gripped him by the upper arms, like Jordon had done so many times to her.

"Beckett." Carlos's body shook with fresh sobs. "He's quitting baseball. He wants me to quit, too. He says that's the only way we can be together." Sounds of sorrow bounced off the walls.

Maggie squeezed her eyes together, mouthing a quick prayer for guidance. "What do *you* want, Carlos?"

"I don't know." He sobbed, and Maggie held him tight. She smoothed his hair and patted his back as she guided him to the living room.

Hard as she tried to come up with one, there was no easy answer.

*

Jordon opened the front door and locked eyes on Maggie wrapped around a teary-eyed Carlos. All the joy he held in his heart at the top of the cul-de-sac dropped to his feet.

"Who jumped in the lake this time?"

It was a bad joke. He admitted it, but he didn't know how else to face the dire expressions.

Carlos blinked and leaped off the couch. He scrambled past Jordon without a word.

"Hey, I was kidding."

Stomping up the stairs over Jordon's head was Carlos's answer.

Jordon released a huffy breath, dropped his carry-on and leveled tired eyes on Maggie. "I thought we were past this."

She rolled her watery eyes and drew her knees to her chest. "We are so not past this."

"Past what?" Honestly, he didn't care. It was selfish, but true. He wanted to pull Maggie into his lap and give her what was pressing against his pants pocket, not deal with more drama.

"Sit." She patted the sofa, but instead of encouraging warmth, the half-hearted gesture and the solemn look on her face colored his mood even colder.

Jordon sat and searched her face for clarity.

She smoothed a hand over his tightening thigh. "Jordon, Carlos is going through…"

"I'm gay," a voice wailed from the loft above Jordon's head.

Jordon looked up to see Carlos leaning over the railing, his face twisted with agony.

"Don't bother throwing me out," Carlos continued through tears. "I'll pack right now. Because I quit!" He disappeared again.

Jordon stared at the empty space as he tried to make sense of the outrageous scene.

"Carlos loves another baseball player named Beckett, and Beckett is quitting baseball. He wants Carlos to quit, too."

The fact that Maggie knew more about this than Jordon shouldn't have come as a surprise. After all, Jordon was paying her to keep the kid's confidence. But Jordon couldn't help wonder if things would've gotten so out of control had he been in the loop sooner.

Anger topped with fear brought him to his feet. "Nobody's quitting anything. Carlos, get down here." He might have roared. At the moment, keeping emotions in check wasn't his top priority.

"Jordon, let him go. He's upset. You're upset. If you talk to him now, you'll say things you'll regret."

Jordon turned toward the lake, afraid that if he turned toward Maggie he would lash out at her. His reflection bounced off the glass. A miserable, twisted face. A furrowed brow. He looked like his old man, someone who refused to see both sides of any situation.

A long, low exhale erased the signs of stress, and Jordon could once again see himself in the reflection. He closed his hand around the turquoise box in his pant pocket, and sighed. All he wanted was five minutes of peace to get down on one knee and ask Maggie to be his wife.

But first, he had to make peace with Carlos.

Jordon turned to Maggie. "You know I can't blindly accept his choice."

Maggie closed the gap between them and wrapped a warm hand around his elbow. "Jordon, he's devastated. Now is not the time to debate whether or not homosexuality is a choice."

"That's not what I'm talking about. I don't care if he's gay. I care if he's quitting. He's twenty. He's too young to throw away his future."

Maggie seemed surprised. She studied him with wide eyes and opened her mouth to speak, but then she pressed her lips together and shook her head.

Maybe Jordon was surprised, too. Carlos was gay. Jordon would've never guessed. Then again, Jordon didn't pry into his players' personal lives. If they asked for advice, he talked. If they supplied information, he listened. Otherwise, what they did off the field was their own damn business. But when what they did off the field threatened what they did on the field, Jordon needed to know.

"He can't make an emotional decision," Jordon continued. "He can't afford to lose his income. He'll be devastated at the loss of reputation. He's…confused, and I won't let him quit."

"But you quit." Maggie's earlier shock was replaced by an

eerie calm, as if she saw the end result and was simply waiting for Jordon to get there.

"Yeah, but I had a plan, a career goal. I didn't give up everything for something stupid like love."

She dropped her chin to her chest and her hand from his arm. "So love is stupid?"

Jordon reached a hand behind his neck and squeezed. "No. I didn't mean it like that...and this isn't about us."

"No. It's not, but let's just say Carlos feels for Beckett what you feel for me. Would you give up everything to be with me?"

"Why are you making this about us?"

She leveled him with dark eyes. "Because I'm trying to get you to relate."

Jordon threw both hands into the air and then pounded them on the top of his head. "Yes! Yes, I would quit for you. I spent the last week shifting clients to associates I know can't do the job as well as me, but I'm cutting back, so I can be with you." Before he knew what he was doing, he'd reached into his pocket and pulled out the box. "Do you want proof? Here's the proof."

She clamped her fingers around his hand before he could open the lid. "Not yet. Wait. Please." She rubbed his knuckles, and his bunching muscles relaxed. "You're right. I'm sorry. This isn't about us. This is about Carlos being stuck between what the world wants him to be and who he wants to be, and we need to help him choose."

Jordon was too upset about Carlos to feel dejected by her brush off, so he stuffed the box back into his pocket with a grind of his teeth. "He's going to lose everything. Do you know how ugly this could get? I can't be a part of that."

The red rims circling her eyes squished until they formed long ovals. "You can't be a part of what? Standing up for a gay man?"

"No! Ruining a career. What if he wakes up one day and decides I failed him? What if he blames me for everything?"

"I won't." Carlos reappeared at the loft railing.

Jordon looked at the miserable kid who was barely a man and tried not to let the frown filling his heart slip onto his face. "It'll be okay, buddy. We'll figure things out."

He didn't know how at first, but then Maggie slid her hand into his, and the minute they touched, he knew...

Now and forever more, they would figure things out together.

CHAPTER SEVENTEEN

Jordon stepped clear of the revolving doors and onto the crowded sidewalk. He darted eyes between hurried commuters to the café across the street.

"Thank you."

Jordon looked at the man by his side. Six months had changed Carlos from a tormented kid to an adult with direction. The extra fifteen pounds of muscle and facial hair didn't hurt either.

Smacking Carlos on the back with a manila folder that held the key to the young man's happiness, Jordon smiled. "You're welcome. Now, show me how thankful you are by throwing a no-hitter tonight."

The men laughed as they dodged traffic to cross the street. Maggie waited for them somewhere along this stretch of sidewalk, and Jordon wouldn't relax completely until she was safe by his side. Not that there was anything to worry about. The doctor said her pregnancy was progressing "beautifully."

Jordon saw her then, chin propped on her hand, eyes focused on her laptop. He didn't know a thing about pregnancies, but he knew beauty. When she looked over the top of her screen, she smiled with her eyes. Rising from her chair, she laid her left hand on the six-month-old bump stretching the material of her blouse. Her large diamond glistened in the sun.

God, how he loved that bump and the woman behind it.

"How'd it go?" she asked.

Jordon pulled her to him before he answered, planting a soft kiss to her neck and breathing in her sweet smell. His hands lingered a little too long on the small of her back, and he found himself counting blocks back to his apartment. It was too far for a pregnant woman to walk. He pulled her closer. They'd call a car.

"It went good. Right, Jordon? Done deal."

Carlos. Jordon forgot. Maggie had that effect on him.

She leaned back and patted him on the shoulder but not before whispering a sultry 'later' in his ear.

Jordon released her, rubbing a possessive hand over the curve of her stomach. "All good. Done deal. May I present to you the newest co-owner of the Morgantown Minors Single-A baseball team, Carlos Nunez."

Maggie squealed and enveloped Carlos in a hug.

"Watch the belly," Jordon warned.

She shot him a teasing glance and settled back into his arms. "It's getting too big to miss."

"And it'll get much bigger. There's a centerfielder growing in there." Jordon waggled his brows at Carlos.

Maggie waved a hand into the space between them. "This child might hate baseball."

The men gasped.

"Well, maybe not hate it, but *she* may turn out to be just like her mother."

Jordon liked the sound of that.

"I've gotta run. Thanks again." Carlos squeezed Jordon's upper arm. "Keep your eyes out for a no-hitter." Carlos winked.

Jordon liked the sound of that too. He watched Carlos flag a taxi and filled with something he imagined was a lot like fatherly pride.

"Do you think anyone suspects anything?" Maggie asked.

"Nope. A lot of team owners are player owners, so nobody suspects Beckett's motives. He was older, on his way out. Retiring and playing minor league ball is a way to lengthen a career." Jordon leaned closer. "And in this case, it's a way for two guys to stay involved without raising suspicions. I'd call that a win-win."

Maggie leaned up and planted a kiss on his cheek, her belly bumping his hip. "You did good, Jordon. I'm proud of you."

He wrapped an arm around her waist. "How proud? Proud enough to race back to the apartment for a quickie before the game?"

Her eyes sparkled. "Who needs an apartment when we have a car with tinted windows?"

She was definitely his soul mate.

*

Carlos didn't throw a no-hitter, but according to Jordon, a one-hitter was sufficient. Maggie had fallen asleep on Jordon's shoulder sometime during the seventh inning and woke with a crick in her neck in time to go home.

Home. In the last six months she'd traveled with Jordon from Charlotte to Tampa to New York and back again. They even managed a house-hunting trip to Idaho. By the end of the year, she could have four houses to call home. To think all she ever wanted was one.

"Why are you still awake?" He wrapped his warm arms around her and pulled her close.

"Why are *you* still awake?" She waited to be chastised with a smile on her face.

Jordon roughed up her shoulder with the scruff on his face. "Oh, no, you don't. I'm on to you. Answering a question with a question is a diversion." He turned his lips to the crook of her neck. "If you want a diversion, I'll give you a diversion."

Maggie laughed and wrapped her arm around his broad shoulder, running her fingernails over his back. "I love you."

He propped on an elbow and traced a fingertip over her jaw. "Say it again."

"I love you." She slid her fingers into the fine hair at the base of his skull and pulled him toward her, brushing her lips over his.

"I love you, too." Jordon smoothed a palm over her sensitive breast, rode the curve of her belly and played along her inner thigh while their mouths sealed their words with a scorching kiss.

He grabbed her around what was left of her waist and urged her into position on top of him. "You are a goddess." His hands roved her swollen body, lighting sparks in the wake of his touch.

She felt like a goddess too, filled with life, filled with him.

The once-empty spaces in Maggie's heart swelled until she thought the muscle might burst from too much happiness. Edging forward to compensate for the heaviness in her chest and belly, Maggie wound arms around Jordon's neck. "You saved me," she whispered.

He chuckled against her cheek. "I think you got that backward, babe."

Nose to nose, Maggie stared into his sparkling eyes. "We saved each other."

Pressing her lips to his, she claimed her future.

ABOUT THE AUTHOR

Elley Arden is a proud Pennsylvania girl who drinks wine like it's water (a slight exaggeration), prefers a night at the ballpark to a night on the town, and believes almond English toffee is the key to happiness. Learn more at *www.elleyarden.com*.

A Sneak Peek from Crimson Romance

On the Fly by Katie Kenyhercz]

LINK on Crimson Website: *http://www.crimsonromance.com/ upcoming-releases-romance-ebook/on-the-fly/*

Chapter One

Thursday, August 25th

Jacey Vaughn clutched a pile of flattened boxes and glanced around the mirrored interior of the elevator. She looked nervous, even to herself, and she swallowed, trying to wipe her slick palms on the cardboard. It felt like waiting to see the dentist. It was late August, which in Las Vegas meant temperatures in the low 90s. Even though the air conditioning hit her full blast, a bead of sweat slid down the back of her neck. When the doors opened, she took a deep breath and stepped off. Twenty pairs of eyes peered at her around cubicles, and she pasted on a weak smile. The glances followed her as she walked down the corridor to her father's office.

A petite, pixie-like woman in her late thirties darted around a desk with a ring of keys. What her light brown hair lacked in length, it made up for in wavy volume. She wore a conservative, gray skirt suit and no makeup but big jewelry. The woman smiled and looked her up and down. "You must be Jacey. I'm Nealy Windham, your father's assistant. Let me get that for you." She jiggled a key in the lock until the door swung open then motioned to the papers strewn across the desk and offered a half smile. "You can't tell now, but it cleans up pretty well. My extension is two-forty if you need anything."

Jacey braced herself, stepped inside, and Nealy saw herself out.

"Change is a good thing," Jacey whispered as she stared at the Stanley Cup Championship plaques lining the wall. They were from the eighties and the Cleveland Rockers incarnation of the current team but still reflected hockey success. The room smelled like the cedar and musk of her father's cologne with a faint undertone of cigar smoke, and she closed her eyes. She could almost feel his presence.

"Hello?"

Jacey gasped, dropped the boxes, and spun around. A man stood in the doorway, solidly built and towered quite a bit over her five feet eight inches, even though she wore heels. He wore a black Las Vegas Sinners T-shirt, cargo shorts to his knees, and leather flip-flops. His gelled blond spikes were styled to look un-styled, and almond-shaped, hazel eyes took her in with no attempt at subtlety. A small, slashing scar at the outside corner of his left eye as well as some purple-yellow bruising under his right told her who he was. Or at least *what* he was. Hockey player.

"Easy there, didn't mean to scare you. I'm looking for Mr. Vaughn."

Her heart contracted at the statement, and she took a slow breath through her nose. When she spoke, there was ice in her voice. "He passed away a week ago." Didn't they know? It was their *owner* who'd died.

The man narrowed his eyes and crossed his arms. "I know. I meant his son, J.C. Vaughn. The new owner of the team."

She bit back a smile, and her cheeks warmed. "I'm Jacquelyn Vaughn. My father...called me Jacey."

He looked her over, but his face gave away nothing. "How much do you know about hockey?"

Jacey straightened. "I know enough. And I have an MBA from Yale, so while I probably couldn't ref a game, I can run the team. You know, I've introduced myself, but you have yet to return the courtesy."

His eyes tightened and an amused smile curled his full lips. "Carter Phlynn, captain of the Sinners."

Her face went slack then she pinched the bridge of her nose. "I'm sorry, I...things happened pretty quickly." When she looked back to him, his sharp features softened, and his arms eased to his sides.

"I understand. I'm sorry about your father."

Jacey pressed her lips together and nodded. Carter turned to go. "Wait. You were looking for me. What did you want?"

He turned back slowly and looked at her for a long moment then shook his head. "Nothing. It can wait."

"No. Please. I could use something to take my mind off of…"

Carter glanced to a spot on the faded burgundy carpet and furrowed his brows. "My agent was in the middle of renegotiating my contract. Your father was also the acting GM after he fired Leyman. I kind of need to know where things stand. I got an offer from the Chicago Blackhawks. My agent should be here any minute."

Jacey's lips parted as that sank in, and it took a minute to find her voice. "You want to leave the Sinners?"

He glanced at her then away again and slid a hand over the back of his neck. "I don't *want* to leave the Sinners. I've played here for the three seasons they've been a team. It's just…Chicago is offering a better deal."

*

Why the hell did he feel guilty? Carter fully intended to play hardball and get the salary he deserved from the Sinners or walk. He'd expected to get in Vaughn Junior's face and come out with no regrets either way. The problem was that Vaughn Junior happened to have big, vulnerable, blue eyes, pouty lips, and legs for days in a skirt that showed them off. And despite the fact she probably couldn't tell a puck from a stick, there was something appealing about her.

She cleared her throat. "If you'll have a seat, I'll look through the paperwork while we wait for your agent."

Carter hesitated, but she moved around the polished oak desk, dropped into a high-backed leather chair—she looked so small— and shuffled through the piles of paper that hadn't been touched. Carefully side-stepping the boxes she'd dropped upon his arrival, he sat in a chair opposite her and leaned back, folding his hands over his stomach.

Carter took in the way her loosely curled, long, strawberry blonde hair was pulled back on top and bet she'd look hot if she let it down. Then he looked away. Hell of a thought when she was grieving for her father. He focused instead on the walls of the office, first noticing a plaque with a team gathered around the Stanley Cup. The Cleveland Rockers had been successful in the eighties but had faded in the following decades.

Next to the plaque, he spotted an old, family 8x10. Everyone in Rockers jerseys. Vaughn Senior in the middle with Jacey under one arm and a young guy under the other. Had to be her brother because they shared the same blue eyes and light hair. Jacey was smiling and happy, but her brother looked sullen, trying to be tough. Carter's eyebrows rose, but he shrugged it off and looked over the cluttered desk, noticing a gold puck with the engraving *Strive for your goals.* Vaughn Senior had certainly believed that.

"I see you've scored the most goals in the past three seasons. More than that, you've had the most assists." Her light blue eyes flashed at him, serious and ensnaring. "You're a team player; I can see why you're captain."

That sounded familiar. When it had been her old man throwing out the compliments, he brushed it off. But coming from Jacey, it sounded sincere. She ducked her head again and flipped through some more papers. If he had to guess, he'd say they were printouts of the team budget. She was actually going to be fair about this. She pulled her lower lip between her teeth and tapped a short, manicured nail against the numbers. Carter caught himself staring and wiped the smile from his face before she could see.

A knock on the open office door jerked him out the trance, and he refrained from telling his agent to leave. It would be counterproductive. Even if he did want a few more minutes alone with Jacey.

"Sorry I'm late. Previous appointment. Brad Curtis. Nice to meet you, Ms. Vaughn. I'm sorry for your loss." Brad extended his hand across Jacey's desk, and they shook.

"Thank you. I was just looking over my father's printouts and notes. From what I can tell, I'm afraid his offer has to stand. I can afford to give Carter another one point five million a year, no more."

"If you'd like to take some time—say, a week—and think things over, talk to your advisors, you can get back to me directly. Mr. Phlynn is in demand, and it would take some incentive to stay with a team that hasn't made the playoffs in its three-year existence." Brad sat in the chair next to Carter's and straightened his suit jacket.

Carter wanted to wince but kept a blank face. His agent hadn't lied about the facts, but it seemed almost cruel to lay it out for her like that.

Jacey nodded once, all business. "I understand, but I know my father. He'd have done anything to make his team the best it could be, and I'm sure that included keeping Carter." Her gaze darted to him and that damn vulnerability shone in her eyes. "If he said one point five million was the best he could do, he meant it. I know you're important to this team, and I'd hate to lose you. Will you stay?"

That question had never gotten an emotional response from him before. Not while picking his clothes up off a date's bedroom floor. Not even when his mother gave him the *my baby* face every time he visited. But damn if he didn't feel bad now. The Blackhawks' offer flashed through his mind. It wasn't so much the money. The Hawks offered him a better chance at the Cup if the past three seasons were any indicator. He glanced up to be once again pinned by that poignant stare. And before he knew what he was doing, he said, "Yeah. Yeah, we have a deal," and stood, extending his hand across the desk. Her small, soft hand felt fragile folded inside his big, callused one, and he smiled. So did she.

"You won't regret this."

His heart clenched.

"Uh, I think we should take a moment and consider—"

"Brad, I appreciate your help, but I'm staying in Vegas for at least one more season." Carter faced his agent and braced for the storm, but Brad contained it. Barely, judging from his clenched jaw and tense posture. Well, he could just deal with it.

*

By 6:05, Jacey had organized all of the documents into color-coded folders. Jack Vaughn's brilliance had not extended to his organizational skills. She ran a hand along the smooth, black leather of the chair and sighed. Having put her things away, she locked her new office door behind her.

Nealy stood and arched her little brows. "Can I help?"

Jacey smiled and shook her head. "Everything's finally in its place. My dad didn't decorate much, so there was room for my things."

Her assistant nodded and skirted her desk to walk beside Jacey toward the elevator.

"It took me three hours just to dig through all the papers and put them in some kind of order. If the figures I found are correct, our budget is very tight. My coach is nowhere to be found, my team captain almost quit, and in raising his salary, I've squeezed the cap even tighter. And this is only the first day."

Nealy followed, huffing a little as she kept up. "What do you mean, 'quit?'"

"He got an offer from the Chicago Blackhawks. After looking at his stats I knew we couldn't lose him, but I couldn't offer any more than my father did. If my research is right, almost *any* other team could afford to give him more, but he decided to stay with us." They stepped into the elevator and stood side-by-side as the doors slid closed.

Nealy frowned, but then a grin slowly spread, and from the corner of her eye, Jacey could almost see the light bulb go on. "What?"

Her assistant hesitated with a smug smile. "Just think about it a minute." Jacey's confusion must have roused pity because Nealy laughed. "Your father gives him the offer. He turns it down. You give him the same offer, and he takes it."

"He seemed like he really just wanted to stay in Vegas..."

"I'm sure he does. Now."

Jacey blew a loose curl away from her forehead. "That's a logical fallacy. Just because B happens after A doesn't mean A caused B."

Nealy held up her hands in surrender, but that smile was still there. "Whatever you say, hon."

The elevator doors opened to the parking garage, and Jacey paused beside her silver Eclipse. The underground air was cooler but not by much. "I can't believe he's really gone."

"Jack Vaughn was a good man and a good boss. He loved hockey, and he loved this team. But more than anything, he loved you and your brother. He talked about you every day."

Jacey felt her heart in her throat, and when she opened her mouth, nothing came out on the first attempt. The second try was a little more successful. "That's...thank you. That's nice to know."

"I know he wasn't an overly affectionate man, but he wasn't shy about his pride for you."

Jacey smiled and wiped at the corner of her eye. "Thank you. I don't know what I'd do without your help."

"S'what I'm here for. Anything you need, let me know."

"Thanks. I'll see you tomorrow, Nealy."

*

Jacey let herself into the hotel room she'd called home for the last week and secured the chain lock behind her. She felt along the wall for the light switch and turned it on. Her suitcases sat along the wall, neatly arranged but taking up a lot of space. Hopefully, that wouldn't be a problem much longer. Turning right to wander into the kitchenette, she opened her fridge to find the carton of skim milk and half of a wrapped, ham and Swiss sandwich. "At least there's not too much to throw away," she mumbled as she drank straight from the carton.

A little red light blinked on the phone by her bed, and she frowned. Considering her day so far, it couldn't be good. Her finger hovered over the button before she gathered the courage to push it.

"Jace, it's me. Look, I'm sorry about what I said in the lawyer's office. I just...Come on. We both thought Dad was leaving me the team. I quit my job."

Jacey rubbed her forehead and closed her eyes. "Madden..."

"The truth is, I know you can handle the team as a business. But let me help. Please. I know I've messed up in the past but...I want us to be close. You're all I have left, Jace." Her brother's voice broke on the machine, and he cleared his throat. "Call me."

BEEP.

She wandered back to the kitchenette with designs on that half-sandwich.

"Ms. Vaughn, this is Coach Tim Finley. I'm sorry to do this, but I can no longer work for the Sinners."

The milk carton fell from her hand and landed with a splat on the linoleum. She stared open-mouthed at the phone.

"Your father and I discussed my salary concerns, but we couldn't come to an agreement. I decided today to accept an offer from a different team. Like I said, I'm sorry. Best of luck with the Sinners."

BEEP.

Frantic, Jacey dug in her purse and found her cell. She searched until she found Finley's number and held it to her ear, barely hearing the ringing over the slamming of her heart. Thank God she'd thought to plug her father's contact list into her phone. As an afterthought, she grabbed a handful of take-out napkins from the counter and bent to sop up the mess.

"Hello?"

"Tim? It's Jacquelyn Vaughn."

"Ah, Ms. Vaughn. Did you get my message?"

Jacey took a silent breath and paused in her cleaning. "Yes, that's why I'm calling. Listen, if you could just coach through the next season, it would be an enormous help—"

"I'm afraid I can't do that; you'll have to find someone else."

Desperation rolled in a wave from head to toe, her chest tightened, and the wet napkins fell from her grip. "But there's no way that I'll find another coach at this short notice."

"I'm sorry, Ms. Vaughn, but I'm set on the matter."

"I understand, but—"

"I'm sorry."

Dial tone.

Jacey leaned back against the cupboards and slumped to the floor. She looked at her phone without seeing it and pushed the *off* button. After a few minutes of inaction, she set it on the counter then returned to the mess on the floor, cleaning on autopilot. An unexpected tear slid down her cheek followed by another and another. She sniffled then laughed. "I'm crying over spilled milk." The laughter mingled with soft sobs and hiccups as she finished the job and wiped her face with the back of her hand.

She stood, kicked off her heels, and belly flopped onto the king-size bed. Face planted in the comforter, arms at her sides, and stocking feet dangling over the edge, she fell fast asleep.

*

Carter slid into McMullan's a little before eight. The bar was already busy with tourists and several regulars. A few heads turned, and he waved and smiled as he weaved his way to a booth in the back, where he found his best friend and goalie, Shane Reese.

Reese's baby face had followed him from pre-teen to post adolescence and guaranteed that he'd get carded well into his thirties. It also gave the goalie a female following that could rival Carter's own. Reese eyed him over a tall mug of beer as Carter slid in the opposite side. "So…?"

Carter slouched back and took a pull from the bottle that had been waiting for him. "I'm staying."

A half smile curled Reese's mouth before he took a drink. He was one of the few men on the team with all his original teeth. A luxury of being a netminder. "Vaughn Junior bend over and beg?"

"I wish."

Reese arched his brows, and Carter smiled devilishly like a kid with a good secret. He leaned his forearms on the table and savored it for a beat. "'Vaughn Junior' wears Chanel Number Five and comes up to my chin in four-inch heels."

Reese feigned a wince. "I hope to God you're talking about a woman."

Carter laughed, nodded, and took another drink.

"And she's hot?"

A reflexive smile escaped before Carter could stop it, and Reese whistled low. An image flashed of Jacey sitting behind the desk doing mental math, and he straightened, clearing his throat. "I mean she's smart, too. Business smart, anyway. Has an MBA from Yale. She doesn't seem to know a lot about hockey, though."

"So how much more are you getting?"

Carter hesitated, shrugged and took a drink. "One point five."

"But…" After a few seconds, the light went on in Reese's eyes. "Damn. Curtis must have shit bricks. You might need to find a new agent."

That could be true. Brad hadn't said a word to him when they left Jacey's office. "Whatever."

Reese didn't seem ready to let it go, but he did and grunted into his mug. Their plate of chili cheese fries arrived. "Peabo really cracked the whip at practice today, man. Worse than Finley. You think Coach'll show up tomorrow?"

The assistant coach, Mike Peabody, definitely had seemed pleased to take over practice. His particular style had been something like military boot camp meets medieval torture. "I don't know. Rumor is he quit."

"You imagine that? Right before we get a new owner."

Carter only nodded.

"You gotta feel bad for Vaughn Junior too. First day on the job, her coach quits and the team captain threatens to walk."

"I didn't *threaten*. And I didn't walk. In fact, I'm taking a pay cut to stay."

Reese's smug expression said he knew why, and Carter ignored it, grabbing a few more chili fries.

"You *like* her." An accusation.

"You weren't there, okay? She had this face and these big, sad eyes, and…"

The goalie smiled.

Carter narrowed his eyes and shook his head. "Shut up, man."

Reese laughed and finished off the fries. "Whatever. We may have been playing together since our Mites days, but you can't tell me you turned down an extra three mil just to see *my* pretty face every day."

"I'm staying. Get over it. We have bigger problems. If Finley did quit, dealing with a new coach is gonna suck."

"I hear ya, brother, but all we can do it hope for the best."

In the mood for more Crimson Romance? Check out *Coming Home* by Christine S. Feldman at *CrimsonRomance.com*.

www.ingramcontent.com/pod-product-compliance
Lightning Source LLC
Chambersburg PA
CBHW010637100726
47900CB00011B/2870